jim thompson
the transgressors

James Myers Thompson was born in Anadarko,
Oklahoma, in 1906. He began writing fiction at a very
young age, selling his first story to *True Detective*
when he was only fourteen. In all, Jim Thompson
wrote twenty-nine novels and two screenplays (for the
Stanley Kubrick films *The Killing* and *Paths of Glory*).
Films based on his novels include: *Coup de Torchon
(Pop. 1280)*, *Serie Noir (A Hell of a Woman)*, *The
Getaway*, *The Killer Inside Me*, *The Grifters*, and
After Dark, My Sweet. A biography of Jim Thompson
will be published by Knopf.

Also by Jim Thompson, available from Vintage Books

the
transgressors

jim thompson

T47315TR

VINTAGE CRIME / **BLACK LIZARD**

vintage books • a division of random house, inc. • new york

First Vintage Crime/Black Lizard Edition, February 1994

Library of Congress Cataloging-in-Publication Data
Thompson, Jim, 1906–1977.
The transgressors / by Jim Thompson. — 1st Vintage Crime/Black
Lizard ed.
p.   cm. — (Vintage crime/Black Lizard)
ISBN 0-679-74016-3
1. Death row inmates—United States—Fiction.   2. Accidents—
United States—Fiction.   I. Title.   II. Series.
PS3539.H6733T7   1994
813'.54—dc20   93-27634   CIP

Manufactured in the United States of America

10   9   8   7   6   5   4   3   2   1

the
transgressors

1

Under the far-west Texas sky, a pale, wind-swept blue in the late August afternoon, the big convertible swayed and swung lazily, jouncing its two occupants—a prostitute and a deputy sheriff—into brief contact; it seemed to crawl toward the horizon like a large black bug, caught inside an up-ended, transparent bowl.

The wind was almost constant, something that one was aware of only when it ceased. The sparse stalks of burned-dry Johnson grass lay almost prone from its pressure, and the giant cacti, the tree-tall Spanish bayonet, leaned warily away from it. It seemed bent on driving everything before it, unwilling to rest until the desolation was absolute.

For the past two-odd hours, ever since they had left the town of Big Sands, the woman had turned in her seat occasionally to look at the man; hopefully at first, then with a kind of frustrated bafflement, and finally with snapping-eyed, tight-lipped fury. Now, at last, she swung abruptly around to stare at him, hiking her skirt high on her thighs, her breasts swelling angrily against her blouse.

The man appeared not to notice. He was, in fact, squinting off to his left, trying to locate the spirelike speck amidst a cluster of lesser specks which, ten miles nearer, would prove to be the derrick and accouterments of a wildcat drilling well.

"Tom . . ." the woman said. "Tom."

The man saw what he was looking for at last. The woman didn't. She was a relative newcomer to the area, still a stranger after almost three years. And strangers here had died of thirst and hunger, of heat or cold, because they accepted the apparent emptiness as real; because, unable to survive themselves, they could not see how others might. They had done it four hundred years ago. They would be doing it four thousand years hence. For the land was unchanging—did not have the necessary elements for change. Men changed it briefly, and then it went back to what it had been.

"Tom! Tom Lord!"

"Yeah, Joyce?"

Deputy Sheriff Tom Lord turned away from the landscape; smiled pleasurably as he noted the hiked-up skirt and the area beneath it. "Oh, gonna take my picture, huh? Want me to say cheese?"

"Stop it! You know what I want!"

"Mmm, let's see," Lord mused—then brigtened exaggeratedly. "Why, sure. Ought to've known right away. Well, you just hop in the back seat and get yourself fixed, an'—"

He broke off abruptly as Joyce Lakewood swung at him.

She swung again, began to pound, claw, and slap at him. His hat, a sixty-dollar ranch-style Stetson fell into the rear of the car. His neat, black bow tie was knocked askew. He ducked and dodged as he drove, sheltering himself with one arm, laughing uproariously and so contagiously that the woman at last joined in. But unwillingly, and not without a trace of bitterness.

"Ah, Tom," she said. "What can I do with you, anyway?"

"Why, now, you've been doing right fine so far," Lord said. "I ain't got a complaint in the world, and that's a fact."

"But what about me? Why did you bring me out here today?"

"You've been saying we needed to have a good long talk," the deputy pointed out. "Can't remember how many times you've said it. Thought we ought to get off some place where we wouldn't be disturbed."

"We wouldn't have been disturbed at my place."

"We-el, maybe not," Lord said. "But I don't reckon we'd have done much talkin'. Seems like we always think of somethin' more interesting to do."

He reached down behind the seat, winking at her slyly as he recovered his hat. Joyce reddened, feeling a mixture of anger and shame.

She was used to vulgarity, to lewdness, to downright filthiness. She had become quite used to it by the time she was fourteen, and she was thirty now. Yet quite often with this man—more and more often, of late—she had found herself blushing at his smallest indelicacy; had been offended and angered and hurt by language which, coming from another man—from any of the hundreds of men before him—would have seemed almost prim.

And she didn't know how to object to it, how to explain why, being what she was, she did object to it. Her only recourse, as now, was to pass over the issue and strike back at a tangent. It would give her no satisfaction, only rebound with more hurt, but still she did it.

"Why do you use that cornball talk?" she snapped. "You're no rube! You're probably the best educated man in the county, practically a medical-school graduate, but you sound like some character in a third-rate movie!"

Lord's delicately arched eyebrows went up. "You mean," he said, "you don't think it's fittin'?"

"Of course it's not! A man who's had your advantages . . ."

"Well, now, looky," Lord cut in, drawling. "Turn it around t'other way, and the same boot fits your foot."

"What—how do you mean?"

"I mean, I'm a heap and I talk like nothin'. You're nothing, and you talk like a heap. Why, y'know," he smiled at her, smiled with his lips and his even white teeth, dark eyes cold and humorless, "as long as you keep a rein on yourself, you could fool almost anyone. Even me, now, I have to keep remindin' myself that you ain't a real honest-to-Gawd lady."

Invariably, when she had tried to pry behind his surface, he had been quick to repel her, but never with such cruelty.

She almost gasped with the pain of it, was far too hurt and humbled to be angry.

"D-do you have to"—she averted her head momentarily, blinking back the sudden tears—"do you have to keep reminding yourself, Tom? Couldn't you just——"

"Well, I guess I don't have to do that," Lord said agreeably. "Not with you always remindin' me yourself."

"I . . . I love you so much, Tom I—I just——"

"An' I think quite a bit of you, too, Joyce. Must've told you so a thousand times."

"But you won't marry me."

"No, ma'am, I sure won't."

"I'm not good enough to marry, but I'm good enough to sleep with. You don't mind sleeping with me, do you?"

Lord said that he didn't mind a-tall. He couldn't think of anything he minded less, and that was a fact. Then, as her face crumbled abruptly, and she burst into helpless, childlike sobs, he dropped his mask for a moment.

"You wouldn't be happy married to me, Joyce. I'm old family. I was reared in a certain way, in a tradition. I couldn't forget it—God knows I've tried to in the past—and I'd never let you forget it."

Joyce raised her head hopefully, all her hurt expunged by this unprecedented gentleness. "Maybe you didn't try hard enough, Tom! You have no real reason to forget, so——"

"Would you say my mother was a real enough reason?"

"What? I don't understand."

"When I was seven years old," Lord said, "she left my

father. Skipped town with another man. Neither Dad nor I ever spoke of her again. As far as we and our friends were concerned, she ceased to exist."

Joyce looked at him, frowning, an unconscious shiver running down her spine. "But—but that's terrible! Didn't you ever hear from her?"

"We received a number of letters from her." Lord took a thin, black cigar from his pocket and ignited the tip. "We destroyed them, unopened."

"But"—the girl fluttered her hands—"she might have been sick, dying! Your own mother dying, for all you know, and . . . and . . . how could you do such a terrible thing?"

"It wasn't easy," Lord said. And then dropping back into his drawl, again sliding behind his mask, "No, sir, it sure wasn't easy, and that's a fact."

He stepped down hard on the accelerator. The big convertible leaped forward, throwing Joyce back against the seat, holding her there with its gathering speed. Faster and faster they sped down the rutted road, bouncing and careening and weaving. She looked at Lord anxiously, started to remonstrate. Then, hesitating, fearful of one of his hide-peeling retorts, she lost the opportunity.

The left front wheel struck a dust-filled chuckhole. The car twisted and jerked, bounced high into the air, and came down with a riflelike *cr-aack*. It whipped sideways, appeared, for a moment, on the verge of flipping over, and then Lord brought it to a stop.

Completely unruffled, he turned and grinned at the white-faced girl.

"Okay, honey? Didn't shake you up none, did I?"

Joyce looked at him wordlessly. She sucked in her breath, sought for some suitable remark—something so cutting and withering that for a time, at least, he would be knocked out of his cocksureness and feel some of the fear and uncertainty that were her own constant companions.

Miraculously, she found exactly the right statement. She began it deliberately, so that none of her words would be lost on him.

"I want to tell you something Thomas DeMontez Lord. I'm well aware that you've got a pedigree as long as my leg, and that I don't amount to anything. But——"

"But it don't matter a-tall," Lord supplied fondly. "To me you'll always be the girl o' my dreams, an' the sweetest flower that grows."

Beaming idiotically, he pooched out his lips and attempted to kiss her. She yanked away from him furiously.

"You shut up! *shu-tt up-pp!* I've got something to say to you, and by God you're going to listen. Do you hear me? You're going to listen!"

Lord nodded agreeably. He said he wanted very much to listen. He knew that anything a brainy little lady like her had to say would be plumb important, as well as pleasin' to the ear, and he didn't want to miss a word of it. So would she mind speaking a little louder?

"I think you stink, Tom Lord! I think you're mean and hateful and stupid, and—louder?" said Joyce.

"Uh-huh. So I can hear you while I'm checkin' the car. Looks like we might be in for a speck of trouble."

He opened the door and got out. He waited at the car side for a moment, looking down at her expectantly.

"Well? Wasn't you goin' to say somethin'?" Then, helpfully, as she merely stared at him in weary silence, "Maybe you could write it down for me, huh? Print it in real big letters, an' I can cipher it out later."

"Aah, go on," she said. "Just go the hell on."

He grinned, nodded, and walked around to the front of the car. Lips pursed mournfully, he stared down at its crazily sagging left side. Then he hunkered down on the heels of his handmade boots, peered into the orderly chaos of axle, shock absorber, and spring.

He went prone on his stomach, the better to pursue his examination. After a time, he straightened again, brushing the red Permian dust from his hands, slapping it from his six-dollar levis and his tailored, twenty-five-dollar shirt.

He wore no gun—a strange ommission for a peace officer in this country. Never, he'd once told Joyce, had he encountered any man or situation that called for a gun. *And he really feels that way,* she thought. *That's really all he's got, all he is. Just a big pile of self-confidence in an almost teensy package. If I could make myself feel the same way . . .*

She studied him hopefully, yearningly; against the limitless background of sky and wasteland it was easy to confirm her analysis. Here in this God-forsaken place, the westerly end of nowhere, Tom Lord looked almost insignificant, almost contemptible.

He *was* handsome, with his coal-black hair and eyes,

his fine-chiseled features. But she'd known plenty of handsomer guys, and, conceding his good looks, what was there left? He wasn't a big man; rather on the medium side. Neither was he very powerful of build. He could move very quickly, she knew (although he seldom found occasion to do so), but he was more wiry than truly strong. And his relatively small hands and feet gave him an almost delicate appearance.

Just nothing, she told herself. *Just so darned sure of himself that he puts the Indian sign on everyone. But, by gosh, I want him and I'm going to have him!*

He caught her eye, came back around the car with the boot-wearer's teetering, half-mincing walk. *Why did these yokels still wear boots, anyway, when most had scarcely sat a horse in years?* He slid in at her side, tucked a cigar into his mouth, and politely proffered one to her.

"Oh, cut it out, Tom!" she snapped. "Can't you stop that stupid clowning for even a minute?"

"This ain't your brand, maybe," Lord suggested. "Or maybe you just don't feel like a cigar?"

"I feel like getting back to town, that's what I feel like! Now, are you going to take me or am I supposed to walk?"

"Might get there faster walkin'," Lord drawled, "seein' as how I got a busted front spring. On the other hand, howsomever, maybe you wouldn't either. I figger it's probl'y a sixty-five-mile walk, and I c'n maybe get this spring patched up in a couple of hours.

"How—with what? There's nothing out here but rattlesnakes."

"Now, ain't it the truth?" Lord laughed with secret amusement. "Not a danged thing but rattlesnakes, so I reckon I'll get the boss rattler to help me."

"Tom! For God's sake!"

"Looky." He pointed, cutting her off. "See that wildcat?"

She saw it then, the distant derrick of the wildcat—a test well in unexplored country. And even with her limited knowledge of such things, she knew that the car could be repaired there; sufficiently, at least, to get them back into town. A wildcatter had to be prepared for almost any emergency. He had to depend on himself, since he was invariably miles and hours away from others.

"Well, let's get going," she said impatiently. "I—" She broke off, frowning. "What did you mean by that rattle-snake gag? Getting the boss rattlesnake to help you?"

"Why, I meant what I said," Lord declared. "What else would I mean, anyways?"

She looked at him, lips compressed. Then, with a shrug of pretended indifference, she took a compact from her purse and went through the motions of fixing her make-up. In his mood, it was the best way to handle him; that is, to show no curiosity whatsoever. Otherwise, she would be baited into a tantrum—teased and provoked until she lost control of herself, and thus lost still another battle in the maddening struggle of Tom Lord vs. Joyce Lakewood.

The car lurched along at a snail's crawl, the left-front mudguard banging and scraping against the tire, occasion-ally scraping against the road itself. Lord whistled tunelessly as he fought the steering wheel. He seemed very pleased with himself, as though some intricate scheme was working out exactly as he had planned. Along with this self-satisfaction, however, Joyce sensed a growing tension. It poured out of him like an electric current, a feeling that the muscles and nerves of his fine-drawn body were coiling for action, and that that action would be all that he anticipated.

Joyce had seen him like this once before—more than once, actually, but on one particularly memorable occasion. That was the day that he had practically mopped up the main street of Big Sands with Aaron McBride, field boss for the Highlands Oil & Gas Company.

Tom had been laying for Aaron McBride for a long time, just waiting to catch him out of line. McBride gave him his opportunity when he showed up in town with a pistol on his hip. He had a legitimate reason for wearing it. It was payday for Highlands, and he was packing a lot of money back into the oil fields. Moreover, as long as the weapon was carried openly, the sheriff's office had made no previous issue of it.

"So what's this all about?" he demanded, when Lord confronted him. "I'm not the only man in town with a gun, or the only one without a permit."

It was the wrong thing to say. By failing to do as he was told instantly—to take out a permit or return the gun to his car—he had played into Lord's hands.

The trouble was that he had virtually had to protest. The deputy had forced him to by his manner of accosting him.

So, "How about it?" he said. "Why single me out on this permit deal?"

"Well, I'll tell you about that," Lord told him. "We aim t' be see-lective, y'know? Don't like to bother no one unless we have to, which I figger we do, in your case. Figger we got to be plumb careful with any of you Highlands big shots."

McBride reddened. He himself had heard that there was ganster money in the company, but that had nothing to do with him. He was an honest man doing a hard job, and the implication that he was anything else was unbearable.

"Look, Lord," he said hoarsely. "I know you've got a grudge against me, and maybe I can't blame you. You think that Highlands swindled you and I helped 'em do it. But you're all wrong, man! I'm no lawyer. I just do what I'm told, and——"

"Uh-huh. An' that could mean trouble with a fella that's workin' for crooks. So you get rid of that pistol right now, Mis-ter McBride. You do that or take you out a permit right now."

McBride couldn't do either, of course. Not immediately, as the deputy demanded. Not without a face-saving respite of at least a few minutes. To do so would make his job well-nigh impossible. Oil-field workers were a rough-tough lot. How could he exert authority over them—make them toe the line, as he had to—if he knuckled under to this small-town clown?

"I'll get around to it a little later," he mumbled desperately. "Just as soon as I go back to the bank, and——"

"Huh-uh. *Now*, Mis-ter McBride," said Lord, and he laid a firmly restraining hand on the field boss's arm.

It was strictly the deputy's game, but McBride had gone too far to throw in. Now, he could only play the last card in what was probably the world's coldest deck.

He flung off Lord's hand and attempted to push past him, inadvertently shoving him into a storefront.

It was practically the last move that McBride made of his own volition.

Lord slugged him in the stomach, so hard that the organ almost pressed against his spine. Then, as he doubled, gasping, vomiting the breakfast he had so lately eaten, Lord straightened him with an uppercut. A rabbit punch redoubled him. And then there was a numbing blow to the heart, and another gut-flattening blow to the stomach . . .

But he couldn't keep up with them. No more could he defend himself against them. He seemed to be fighting not one man but a dozen. And he could no longer think of face-saving, of honor, but only of escape.

Why, he's going to kill me, he thought wildly. *I meant him no harm. I've given willful hurt to no man. I was just doing my job, just following orders, and for that he's going to kill me. Beat me to death in front of a hundred people.*

Somehow more terrible than the certainty that he was

about to die was the knowledge that Lord would probably not suffer for it: the murder would go unpunished. He, McBride, would be cited as in the wrong, and he, Lord, would go scot-free, an officer who had only done his duty, though perhaps too energetically.

McBride staggered into the street, flopped sprawling in the stinging dust. Fear-maddened, fleeing the lengthening shadow of death, he scrambled to his feet again. He couldn't see; he was long past the point of coherent thinking. Dimly, he heard laughter, hoots of derision, but he could not read the racket properly. He could not grasp that Lord had withdrawn from the fight minutes ago, and that his leaden arms were flailing at nothing but the air.

He hated them too much to understand—the people of this isolated law-unto-itself world that was Lord's world. This, he was sure, was the way they *would* act; laughing at a dying man, laughing as a man was beaten to death. And nothing would be done about it. Nothing unless . . .

Donna! Donna, his young wife, the girl who was both daughter and wife to him. Donna was like he was. She lived by the rules, never compromising, never blinded or diverted by circumstance. And Donna would——

When he regained consciousness he was in Lord's house, in the office of Doctor Lord, the deputy's deceased father. Lord had been ministering to him, bathing his face, treating his many cuts and bruises with a variety of medicines.

"Don't worry," Lord grinned at him genially as he opened his eyes. "I won't mess you up none. Never got a degree, but I probably know more medicine than my Dad did."

McBride tried to get up. Lord pressed his chest gently, holding him on the lounge.

"Right sorry about our little scuffle," he went on. "Just couldn't see no way out of it, y'know? Had to show you that if one fella starts misusin' the law, another'n can do the same thing."

"So it was strictly a personal matter!" McBride said bitterly. "You didn't care whether I had a gun permit or not! You——"

"Ain't everything personal?" Lord asked. "Any way of doin' somethin' that isn't? You pulled this swindle on me, and it's just business with you. There's nothing personal in it. But——"

"I negotiated an agreement with you for my company! An entirely legal agreement!"

"Uh-huh. An' I give you a beating in the interests of this county—an entirely legal beating. But it don't make you feel no better, does it?" The deputy leaned forward earnestly. "Now, looky, McBride. I didn't make any deal with your company. I made it with you, and it's your responsibility to straighten it out—to try to anyways. If you'd just try, it . . ."

McBride wasn't listening to him. It would have made no difference if he had. In his struggle upward through the ranks, he had never belonged to a union. Insofar as he had a viewpoint, it was always identical with his employer's.

He was rigidly honest; that is, he had never broken a law. It was no concern of his if, as the instrument of his company, he perverted the law. There was a loser and a winner in every transaction. It was McBride's job—his creed, his religion—to see that his employers were not the losers.

Now, with Lord in midsentence, he arose determinedly and announced that he was leaving. "Unless you plan on giving me another beating. You've proved that you can do it."

"But—but wait a minute," Lord frowned. "We can't just leave things like this."

"That depends on you. I'll never show my face in Big Sands again; I couldn't after today. I'll keep out of your way, you keep out of mine. Because if you don't, Lord, if you ever stick your nose into my business without proper authority . . ."

"Yeah? If I ever stick my nose into your business?"

"I'll blow it for you. Right through the back of your head."

Lord laughed softly. "Now, maybe I'll give you a crack at doin' that," he said. "Yes, sir, I just may do that."

McBride did not appear in Big Sands again, going instead to another town that was twenty miles farther away. As far as his job was concerned, he was never able to completely reassert his authority. He fired a dozen men. He whipped as many others. But something had died inside of him, and he could not revive it. He went nowhere unless he had to. He talked to no one unless he had to. He withdrew deeper and deeper into himself. And he brooded.

He brooded.

Joyce Lakewood looked up from her compact as the convertible swung bumpily to the right. They were turning into the prairie, multitracked at this point by the treads of tractors, trucks, and other vehicles. Ahead of them, perhaps a mile, were the derrick and outbuildings of the drilling well. Here at roadside was a sign.

To the uninitiated, it might have seemed ludicrously prolix. But in oil country it was commonplace, differing only in its details and their arrangement from innumerable thousands of such signs.

It read:

T. DeM. Lord Survey
Pardee Co., Elsin. Township
So. 160, N.E. Sect., Lots 16–30
Test No. 1
HIGHLANDS OIL & GAS COMPANY
Aaron McBride, Supt.

2

Joyce's eyes widened. White-faced, she grabbed Lord's arm. "Tom stop! You can't go up there!"

"You say you saw a bear?" Lord cupped a hand on his ear interestedly. "I don't hear so good, honey."

"You heard me, damn you!" Joyce yelled. "Aah, please, Tom. Don't——"

"It ain't perlite to stare? Spring is in the air?" Lord persisted; and then, seeing that she was on the verge of tears, he patted her reassuringly on the knee. "Now, what you in such a sweat about? Highland's runnin' a flock of rigs. No reason why McBride'd be at this one."

Joyce angrily asked who he thought he was kidding. This was a test well, a very special job. The chances were better than even that the field boss would be here.

"And you know it! Why—why, I'll bet you broke that spring deliberately! Just to give yourself an excuse to start something!"

"Aw, naw!" Lord protested. "You don't really think I'd do a thing like that?"

"All right," Joyce said tiredly, "I give up. If you insist on getting your head shot off, I can't——" She broke off, pointing, her face brightening with relief. "Well, maybe McBride won't be here after all. It looks like the well's shut down."

Lord agreed that she was right, praising her perceptiveness, adding that he would never have observed the fact himself if he had been stone blind, deaf, or more than five miles away. From this she gathered correctly that he had noticed the lack of activity and noise minutes ago, perhaps at the time the car spring was broken.

"But there's someone here," she said quickly. "Those men coming out of the bunkhouse. Isn't one of them——?"

"Naw. Them's Red Norton an' Curly Shaw. Couple of friends o' mine."

Joyce supposed that they probably were friends if he could call them by name—and he could do the same with hundreds of men. People sort of kept their distance around Lord, or rather they were kept at a distance. But they liked him, and he exuded a feeling of liking them.

"But please, Tom," she urged, "don't stall around here. Just get the spring fixed, if we can get it fixed, and clear out fast."

"Why sure. Sure, I will," Lord said. "Won't linger no more than a weasel in a henhouse."

He stopped the car, got out, then teetered forward as the two men advanced to meet him. They met about fifteen feet from the convertible. They shook hands, inquired into the state of one another's health, and made elaborately detailed comments about the weather.

Joyce sighed and rolled her eyes. What *was* the matter with him, she thought. What was the matter with everyone out here? They couldn't even go to the toilet without making a ceremony out of it.

She listened nervously to their laconic talk, wondering why the hell Tom didn't get down to business. Point out the broken spring to them, and ask for help in repairing it. Instead of that he was gabbing on about everything under the sun—just stalling on death's doorstep, with McBride apt to show up at any minute!

In the viewpoint of the three men, of course, their conduct was exactly as it should be. It was obvious that the car had a broken spring. Why insult a man's intelligence by pointing it out, or reflect on his courtesy by asking for help? Help would be given—since there was no place else to get it—as soon as it could be; as soon as certain concomitant problems had been worked out in the giver's mind. Meanwhile, here were three friends come together, and there were obligations to be observed on such an occasion.

In this sparsely settled area, a man might go months without seeing a friend or even another man. And, naturally, when there was a gap in the long loneliness, it would not be closed in haste. Indeed, it could not be. For how could a man live if he took no interest in others, or others in him? What reason did he have to live?

Lord passed the cigars, and held a match for his friends. When theirs were lit, he fired his own with another match, pinched the flame out with his fingers, and flicked it idly toward the drilling rig.

"Little trouble?" he asked.

"Quite a little," said Curly Shaw; and Red Norton explained that a string of tools had been lost down the hole.

"Like to take a look, Tom?"

"Well—" Lord hesitated, then realized that the invitation was a suggestion. This, apparently, was something that concerned him. "Why, yeah," he said, rising from his hunkers. "Might be something to see."

It was a cable-tool rig, a kind of drilling machine as old as the industry itself. It "made hole" by lifting and dropping a heavy drill bit. In the last decade or so, it had lost much of its popularity to the rotary rig, which drills by whirling its bit and is considerably faster. But in an unexplored and extremely isolated area such as this—where no more than one well might be drilled—it had seemed unwise to haul in and set up so much complex and expensive machinery.

Standing on the ground near the derrick floor, Tom Lord looked up into the rig. The drill tools—the "string" composed of stem, jars, and bit—were missing. About forty feet up, the bare cable dangled lazily in the wind.

Red Norton explained what had happened. "Around nine hundred feet down at this point. Set our twelve-inch pipe yesterday noon at eight-fifty, and went on drilling until about four. Then the structure got awful soft on us, began havin' a hell of a time pulling out. McBride figured we'd better under-ream . . ."

Lord nodded. In very soft structure, an under-reamer replaces the drill bit. By working inside the pipe—which follows it down into the ground, instead of remaining stationary—it makes hole without the danger of cave-ins and the costly delays and fishing jobs incident to them.

"So?" the deputy prompted.

"So all our other rigs is rotary, and we couldn't get an under-reamer trucked in before tomorrow. McBride figured we'd better wait for it; he don't take no chances, you know. So he fires us all, and the other tower [crew] took off. Me and Curly figured we'd better stick—give us a place to sleep anyway."

Lord looked dismayed. "He fired you—just because you wasn't needed for a day or so?"

"Why not?" Curly said grimly. "Plenty of cable-tool men out of work. Pick 'em up any time."

"Well, anyways," Norton went on. "We come out this morning, and that"—he pointed with his cigar—"that's what we found. Cable cut. About six thousand pounds of tools jammed down there in the guck."

Lord said, "Do tell," adding by way of good measure, a "tsk, tsk." Then as the subsequent silence deepened: "You sure the cable was cut? Couldn't have happened no other way?"

Norton shrugged. "I reckon. It don't seem likely, though, and McBride don't think it was."

"Uh-*huh*," Lord said, "and I bet he thinks he knows

who done it. Some fella close enough for you to spit on."

"Look, Tom," Curly said. "Why don't you take me'n Red's car and leave yours here? We ain't going nowheres."

"Well—" Lord considered the offer and refused it with thanks. "McBride finds my car here an' yours gone, you'd be in a bad way with him. Wouldn't want no one around that liked me that well. Now, if you'll just give me the lend of a couple spring leaves——"

"We can't, Tom. McBride's got everything locked up, even to the cookhouse." Curly spat scornfully. "Got a lot of faith in folks, you know. Prob'ly trust his mother with her own milk."

He repeated the proffer of the car, and was again refused. Lord asked when the field boss was due back.

"Can't be a whole lot longer," Curly said. "We ain't had nothing to eat since breakfast, and he's going to tick us for a little grub. Actually lettin' us have something to eat until we're back on the payroll again."

Lord deliberated, and came to a decision. He explained it to his two friends, and they agreed to it. They had to, according to their code. They would have felt bound to, even if Lord had been a stranger.

He hallooed to Joyce, gestured, and pointed. Starting the car, she drove slowly toward them. Meanwhile, as she approached the toolshed platform, Lord pried open the shed door.

"Now, this is all on my head," he reiterated, as he rolled the chain hoist out on its track, "an' I'll be plumb sore if you fellas shoulder any blame for it. I broke the door open.

I took the stuff I needed. All you did was take the money I'll leave with you, and I'll leave plenty to cover the damages. You-all didn't have anything to do with it, and there wasn't nothin' you could do about it."

They went to work quickly, hooking under the front of the car and hoisting it upward. Then, while Joyce squatted on a timber a few feet away, anxiously watching their progress, all three hustled out the broken spring leaves and forced the new ones into place.

There was a great deal of clamor, banging and scraping, and cursing (the last subdued because of a "lady's" nearness). Due to the tip-tilted position of the car, they could not see beyond it.

Thus, they did not hear McBride's approach. And he was only a few feet away when they saw him.

He held a gun in his hand. He gestured with it, motioning Curly and Red to one side. Then, he took aim at Tom Lord.

3

It was in the spring of Lord's second year in medical school that he was forced to drop out. His father's serious illness, and the consequent shortage of funds, forced his return home. The hiatus, he was confident, would be brief. He would be back in school by fall, at the latest, working doubly hard to make up for the time he had lost.

He just about had to, you see. It was impossible to contemplate any other course.

Unfortunately, the elder Lord did not recover as expected. It was equally unfortunate—though Tom, of course, did not consider it so—the old gentleman did not die. He simply lingered on year after year, needing more and more attention, requiring more and more money to maintain the life that was no longer worth living.

The house was mortgaged, then the furniture. Hard-pressed debtors scrimped and scraped to pay the doctor his overdue due. Others—self-proclaimed debtors—hurried to pay their fictitious bills. The bank could not lend more money, but the bank president himself did. Local merchants extended unlimited credit, and slashed their bills in half.

None of this munificence was considered charity. Everyone knew that Tom Lord knew what was happening, and would eventually settle his debts in full. For the Lords were *people* as distinguished from mere people. They would prove it, when the tide turned, just as the other *people* of the county were proving it now.

A job? Some way for Tom Lord to earn his keep, and climb out of the hole where fate had thrust him? Well, sure. You name a job that they could give him, and Tom Lord could have it. But just what was there to give? What was there for a young man of old family—but without means—to do out here in this hundred-million-acre pasture?

Couldn't have him playing ribbon clerk. Couldn't expect him to punch cows for forty and found. Such jobs just wouldn't have been fitting, and they were rarely available, anyway. Yet when you'd named them, you'd practically named them all.

Back in the beginning, when the message seemed only of academic interest, Tom had seen the handwriting on the wall. There was nothing here for such as he; not without a profession or business. He had known then that he must finish his schooling, or else. And now, at last, he was forced to face the else.

Seven years after he had dropped out of college his father died. When Sheriff Dave Bradley called to pay his respects, Tom took him apart from the other mourners.

"I hear you've got a deputy opening," he said simply. "I'd like to have the job."

Bradley seemed both stunned and embarrassed by the announcement. He pointed out that he liked to have a man perm'nent, whereas Tom would soon be heading back to school.

"I won't be. Even if I had the money, it would be out of the question. I've been out too long. I'd practically have to begin all over."

"But a deppity job . . ." Bradley protested. "Ain't nothin' wrong with it, of course. Takes a man t'hold it, and the pay's pretty good for these parts. But—but . . ."

"I see. You're thinking I wouldn't fit in with your other men. I'd act in a way they'd resent."

"Well"—Bradley squirmed—"you wouldn't mean to, of course. Know it ain't like you to be uppity. But——"

"Now, looky, Sheriff Dave," Tom drawled, "gimme a chance, huh? You just gimme a chance, an' there won't be no kicks. Those men o' your'n'll cotton to me like burrs to a dog fox."

"Like I was sayin'," the sheriff continued. "You wouldn't"——He broke off, his eyes popping in a wide double take. "What'd you say, boy?"

"I mean it," Tom grinned. "I'll fit in, an' that's a fact. Won't stand out no more'n a fly turd in a box of pepper."

He got the job, and he kept it. It was easy, frighteningly easy. Descent always is. It had taken centuries of fine breeding, plus a small fortune, to make him what he was. It took less than a year to completely unmake him, to put him on the level with half-literate "courthouse cowboys," men who made a boast of ignorance and were warily suspicious of its opposite.

Superficially, that is, the change took no longer than that. Actually, the transformation never took place. For behind—inside—the drawling, doltish Tom Lord, there was another, the real man. The Lord of the conquistadores, the Lord who could not live the role he was cast in and was unmercifully denied the right to die.

He, the real man, became smaller and smaller as the years went by, and the outer shell became thicker. But he was there, all right. A little of him was constantly poking through to the surface, showing up in exaggerated Westernisms and savagely sly gibes—blindly, bitterly striking back at the world he could not change.

Shrewd old Dave Bradley noticed, and spoke to him about it. Was he feelin' kind of mean, huh? Was he kind of sore at folks gen'rally, windin' up to give 'em a boot the first time he caught 'em squatting?

Tom seemed baffled by the question. Just couldn't cipher out what Sheriff Dave was diggin' at. "Why, what have I got t'be riled about? Looks to me like I got just about everything a man could ask for. The county takin' care of me, an' a swell bunch of fellas to work with—always funnin' and grab-assin'—and nothin' at all to fret my mind. Nothin' that calls for any thinkin'. No real work, you might say, just keepin' myself handy and lookin' pretty, like I wouldn't pee if my pants was on fire."

Bradley chuckled unwillingly. "Now, boy. I——"

"You think I'm jokin'?" Lord said. "Why, looky, Dave. Here I am only thirty-three years old, an' I'm deppity sheriff in a county of danged near nineteen hundred population. No tellin' how far I'll go in the next ten years!"

"You might," said Bradley, "go further than you think."

"Says which?"

The sheriff explained. The oil fields were edging toward Pardee county. Already more people were drifting in. "I ain't too active no more, Tom. I could use a chief deputy. It'd be quite a bit better'n you got now, an' when I step out you'd have the job cinched."

"Me? Me sheriff of the whole county!" Tom was obviously stunned by the glorious prospect. "Why, I'm plumb tongue-tied, Dave! Just don't hardly know what to say."

"You got plenty of time to think of somethin'," the sheriff pointed out drily. "Might be you won't need to think of nothin' at all."

He was hurt. Lord was quickly contrite. "I'm sorry, Dave; it's just a habit I've slipped into. I'm not man enough to fill your boots, and I'd never have the heart to try. But I'd surely like to be your chief deputy."

"Well, now," Bradley said as he cleared his throat noisily, "can't think of a man I'd rather have, when it comes to that. But, Tom—Tom, boy"—over his glasses, he shot Lord a steel-blue glance—"watch yourself, huh? You got something eatin' you. Drag it out in the open. Don't let it take over with you."

"I'll watch it. I won't let it take over," Lord promised.

"You do that. Because there ain't nothing uglier than a law man turned mean. He's back behind his badge, and the common folks're out in front of him. Kinda got the world by the tail, y' know. Just pinchin' it a little to begin with, then swingin' it. An' then taking a try at poppin' its neck."

The other deputies also noticed Lord's clownish gibing, but they could not see it as that—without regarding themselves as ridiculous—nor did they interpret it for what it was. Tom was just tryin' to be friendly, that was all. Just tryin' to be one of the boys. And if he maybe worked a little too hard at it, you couldn't fault a man for that. Why old Tom was one of the finest fellas you'd want to meet: always ready for a pint or a poker game, and plen-ty man besides. Don't let the way he looks fool you, mister. There's a fella that c'd hunt bears with a switch.

Far from being envious, they were pleased and proud of his eventual appointment as chief deputy. Ol' Tom had it coming to him, if anyone did, and it was best all around that he should have it. If you'd picked one of them, now, one of the old-line deputies, the others would have been sore. But with Tom having a little somethin' extra, it was all right. Made things pretty nice, any way you looked at it. Tom never hit you in the face with his learnin'—just talked an' acted like anyone else—but don't think he didn't have it! Prob'ly the smartest man this side of the Pecos. And having a fella like that for chief deputy, well, it was plumb nice. Sort of made everything classier, like Pardee County was really comin' up in the world.

So everyone was happy about Tom Lord's new job. Everyone was content with his tenancy of it.

Everyone, that is, but the tenant himself.

He knew, by now, that far-west Texas must be his home forever. He had spent too much of his life here, become too much a part of the land and its people, to adapt to another place. And that was all right. He liked it here. He only disliked his existence here—the insistent necessity to be what he was not. Perhaps, if he was allowed to choose, if he had a free choice of being what he was or being something else, then the status quo would be tolerable. He might even decide to continue it.

But to have no choice, to be force-fed with a way of life, to have to sneak and crawl inside a tightening shell . . . .

It was not too late to break out of it. The desire to do so was still in him. Only one thing was needed: money. And where a fellow like him was going to lay his hands on any real money . . . .

Out of the dead and buried past, a voice whispered to him, whispered that the money could be had. It had been almost three decades since he had last heard that voice, almost thirty years since its owner had walked out of his life, with an impenetrable wall rising up behind her. But now she spoke to him again; hazily, he relived the brief moments of their long-ago parting:

The perfume . . . the moonlight drifting through the window . . . the cottonwood trees rustling in the wind . . . and a tiny gloved hand gently urging him to wakefulness:

And he, peevishly, "What you want, Mama? What you all dressed up for?"

"Ssh, darling. I want you to take this. Take very good care of it. It's a-all—all I have to give you, and——Here: I'll put it in your chest for you, right under your Tarzan books."

"What is it, Mama? Where you goin'?"

"Never mind. You'll understand when you're older. Just take good care of it, and don't tell a soul about it."

"I can tell Papa, can't I?"

"No! He'd just laugh—call it a lot of nonsense. Anything I do or say, he'd . . . You mustn't tell him, anyway. You'll understand that later, too."

"Mama, where you——?"

"You go back to sleep now. Hurry like a good boy, and I'll stay here with you."

And, he, brightening. "Yes'um. G'night, Mama."

And she, very softly, her voice blurring into this slumber, "Good-bye, my darling . . ."

It was all still where she had put it, the thin parchment package wrapped in endless layers of rotting silk.

Tom exhumed it, and took it to a lawyer. Then, feeling pretty silly about the whole thing, telling himself that of course there was nothing to it, he sat back to await the verdict.

The lawyer was in his dotage, and he had never been much good to begin with. There had been no practice here to make him so, and being one of the *people,* as Tom was, he could exist comfortably in mediocrity.

His attitude, as he began to read the parchment, was anything but encouraging.

Another one of these things, huh? Yeah, he'd seen plenty of 'em in his time; used to be about as common as buried-treasure maps. See some Mex sheepherder, and you could just about bet beans to biscuits that he had one of the things in his bindle.

He frowned suddenly, squinted. He took off his glasses and polished them, then bent so close to the document that his beak nose brushed against it.

"Well, I'll be danged," he breathed. "Yes, sir, I will be danged!"

"Yes, sir?" Tom prompted.

"Hesh up, can't you? You're in such an all-fired hurry you c'n go somewheres else."

"Yes, sir," said Tom meekly.

The lawyer fingered the parchment with almost loving delicacy. Taking a large magnifying glass from his desk, he scanned its faded, spidery lettering.

At last he leaned back in his chair and shook his head wonderingly.

"You got yourself somethin' there, son. Looks like you're about the biggest landowner in the county."

"Honest?" Tom's face cracked into a grin. "You really mean it?"

"Somethin' wrong with your ears? I said so, didn't I?" The lawyer eyed him sternly before continuing. " 'Course it's the worst land in the county, which makes it just about the most no-account in the world. Grasshopper couldn't cross it unless he carried his lunch with him. But the mineral rights, now—if the oil boom should swing your way . . ."

"Holy God," Tom mumured reverently. "Hot jumpin' Hannah! I—You're sure about it, sir? I'm not doubting your word, but——"

"Sounds t'me like you are! Sounds like you think I don't know my business. Prob'ly make yourself a million dollars an' give me the go-by for some young smart-aleck lawyer."

"Now, I wouldn't do that, sir," Tom said quietly. "Any business I have, you can handle it for me. And I'd be right hurt if you didn't take it."

The lawyer was mollified, even moved to a senile tear or two. He assured Tom that he would have plen-ty of business—*if* there was oil on his holdings.

"This here's a Royal Spanish Land Grant, son. Highest courts in the country have upheld 'em. That land's yours just as if old Ferdinand and Isabella had give it to you their-selves. Which," he cackled shrilly, pointing to the signatures on the parchment, "is just what they went and done!"

In due time, the oil boom crept into Pardee County. The oil fields swung toward Tom Lord's land. Not all of it, but large sections of it; enough to assure him that his fortune was made, and that his only concern need be the amount of it.

An uninterrupted procession of lease hounds, scouts, executives, and independent entrepreneurs called on him.

Their offers ranged from fair to foolish, from middling bad to excellent-plus. Tom Lord, in concert with his lawyer, gave them all the same short shrift.

"Ain't gonna let a client of mine get cheated," the lawyer declared. "How do we know what's under the ground, hah? All we know is it's our'n and we're entitled to it, minus a fair share for gettin' it to the surface."

That sounded reasonable and right to Tom Lord, but he was getting a little nervous. After all, there are no underground surveyor's stakes, and no oil field, however rich, is inexhaustible. His land could still be drained dry, even though there were no wells on it. The wells on surrounding property would siphon it off.

Lord's nervousness was getting hard to live with when he was offered exactly the kind of deal his lawyer demanded. The man who made it to him was Aaron McBride.

He liked McBride instantly, liked his direct speech and economy with words. He liked the simple contract that McBride tendered him, a document that was almost terse in its simplicity, and completely devoid of irritating legalisms.

For a flat twenty-five per cent of Tom's holdings, McBride's employers—Highlands Oil & Gas—would undertake all production costs. This twenty-five per cent would cover the drilling of wells, the laying of pipelines, the setting up of storage tanks—everything that needed to be done to market the oil. Tom would have no expenses whatsoever, and seventy-five percent of the oil would be his. Or, more accurately, one hundred per cent of the oil would be his on the *seventy-five per cent of the land remaining to him*.

It sounded good to Lord. It sounded equally good or better to his lawyer.

Still, even as the lawyer pressed a pen into his hand and pointed to the dotted line, he found himself drawing back. So very much depended on this. Not mere money, but the very life of a man.

He slowly looked up from the contract, and into McBride's eyes.

"Should I sign this or not, Mr. McBride?" he asked. "You tell me I should, that it's a good contract, and I'll sign it."

"I'm not a lawyer," McBride said.

"That's not what I asked you."

"But, man—" McBride began a protest— "you're asking me to—to——" He broke off, reached into his pocket, and took out a certified check for twenty thousand dollars. He shoved it cross the desk and leaned back. "There," he said, "I wasn't suposed to give you that if you'd sign without it. But—well, now, I feel better."

"And so do I," said Tom warmly. "Always thought you were on the level. Now, I know it."

And he signed the contract.

He bought his convertible with a fraction of the money. The rest was promptly absorbed by attorney's fees and his old debts.

Wisely, he held onto his job. For the twenty thousand dollars was the only money he ever received.

When his first suspicions arose, he was ashamed of them. He chided himself with impatience, told himself that McBride was a very busy man and that any seeming wrong would be righted as soon as McBride could get around to it.

McBride had proved his honesty, hadn't he? And he certainly was busy, wasn't he? Tom had hailed him a time or two, approached him with the intent to talk over his situation if the opportunity presented. But he could never get past a polite feeler or so before McBride was forced to rush away.

A very busy man, the field boss. Still, Tom thought, this *was* business, the matter that he wished to discuss. It was very big business, and he was entitled to a few minutes of McBride's time.

The few minutes were not easy to obtain. He only got it, after three days of pursuit, by pulling his car in front of McBride's.

The field boss scowled as Lord came tramping back to his vehicle. He said, as Lord climbed into the seat with him, that he didn't think he liked this. He didn't like it at all, and he didn't have to put up with it.

"Sure, you don't," Tom agreed. "But I figured maybe you'd want to. You got a choice of doin' this or something else, and I got a notion you'd be happier doing this."

McBride hesitated, seeking some means of equivocation and finding none. At last, he said curtly, "All right. We signed our agreement approximately a year ago. Now, you're wondering when we're going to drill on the seventy-five per cent of the lease land owned by you."

Lord nodded. "Can't blame me for that, can you? seein' that you've sunk more than fifty wells on your twenty-five per cent."

"The answer is that I don't know."

"No idea, huh? You're the field boss. You've got to plan a long ways ahead, keep all your rigs and men working with no lost motion. But you got no notion of when you'll drill on my property."

McBride's mouth tightened doggedly. He said nothing.

"The fact is," Lord said, "you won't be puttin' down no wells at all on my seventy-five per cent. That's about the size of things, ain't it? There won't be nothin' but offset wells, taking all the oil for Highlands and givin' me nothing."

"I didn't say that."

"But you know it's true. You knew it right in the beginning. Now, I'm asking you to make it square with me."

"I—How do you mean?"

"Go before a judge with me. Just tell what you know—what you got to know. That the contract was made in bad faith with intent to defraud."

"But I—" McBride hesitated, swallowed heavily. Then, he continued in flat, dull tones, seeming to recite from some carefully memorized lesson in a distasteful subject. "You had a lawyer," he said. "The contract was entirely legal. It was not my job to interpret its contents."

Lord gave him a long, thoughtful look. Slowly he took out a cigar and lighted it. "This legal stuff," he said. "I always felt it was meant to protect people. Might go astray now and then; ain't perfect no more than the people that use it. But if it did, you could pick it up again an' pry things back on the track. That's what I was askin' you to do . . ."

He waited, taking another puff from the cigar. McBride was silent, his hands clutching the steering wheel tightly, his eyes fixed straight ahead.

"Been a lot of people like you around," Lord went on, "right from the beginning of history. Burnin' and torturin' and killing—slappin' other people into the gas ovens. And it's always done legal, y'know. They always got a law to back 'em up. If there ain't one on the books, someone'll think one up in a hurry. Anyways, they're just followin' orders, ain't they? It's no skin off their nose if——"

"Mr. Lord!" McBride's head snapped around. "I was a combat infantryman during World War II! I spent one year in a German hell camp!"

"And I guess it didn't learn you a thing," Lord said sadly. "Didn't teach you that a man's got certain obligations to do what's right, regardless of whether it's convenient or what the law will let him get away with. Well"— he opened the car door and paused as he slid from the seat—"I guess I'll just have to plug up a few holes in your ed-u-cation, Mis-ter McBride. Looks like it was my bounden duty."

He nodded, grinning coldly, and departed.

It was two weeks later that, having caught McBride without a gun permit, and McBride having "resisted arrest," he beat him insensible.

*   *   *

And now he was face to face with McBride again. And McBride's gun was aimed at him.

And McBride, obviously, was more than prepared to use it.

All he needed was a reason, an excuse, the slightest provocation or justification.

Perhaps, judging by the half-crazed look in his eyes, he did not even need that.

4

In retrospect, it seemed to Tom Lord that there were a dozen ways that he could have handled the situation, any of them better than the one he chose. But that was later. At the time, he was not even conscious of making a choice; what he did was inevitable, a course that was thrust upon him. At the time he could think of only one thing: that he had made the biggest mistake of his life in coming here. That he should never have come here, regardless of his need to, or of his nagging anger with McBride.

The facts were, of course, that he would not have done so if he had been aware of the severed cable and the drill tools lost down the hole. He would have realized that McBride would blame him for the disaster, that he would take this—a seeming attack on his, McBride's, work and company responsibilities—every bit as hard as, or harder than, he had taken the beating.

But Lord hadn't known about the lost tools. And there was no way now to compensate for this vital bit of ignorance.

He should have got away from the place faster. He simply shouldn't have been there to begin with.

"I want to tell you something," Lord heard himself saying. "I didn't cut your drill cable. I can prove that I was in town all last night."

McBride's lips drew back from his teeth in a broad, humorless grin. He laughed a high-pitched cackling laugh.

"Yes, you can," he said. "I'm sure of it. You'd lie and the whole town would swear to it."

He had aged ten years since the beating, Lord saw. He had lost almost forty pounds. He was haggard and deathly sick-looking, a man disintegrating under the conflicts of his job and his conscience. Lord had made him see the basic wrong of his existence, the only one he had ever lived or was capable of living. And because Lord had done so, and because he himself could not accept the responsibility, it became Lord's fault.

Everything. All of it . . . That woman in the compensation court, where he had testified for the company. That Negro 'cropper, watching dully as the huge tractors rolled through the family burial plot. The way his men looked at him. The way his dead wife had treated him. The . . . *the starved bodies hanging in the barbed wire, and the long trench with the bubbling quicklime and the smell of roasting flesh, and . . .*

"I had a broken spring on my car," Lord said very slowly, letting each word sink in. "I had to come here for help. I was going to pay for everything I used or broke."

McBride let out another high-pitched cackle. He said

that, of course, that was the way it was and that was what Lord had intended to do. It was a lie, but Red and Curly and the woman would swear to it.

"You," he said, his voice suddenly sharp, slanting a glance at the two workmen. "You've drawn your pay. Now I'll give you ten minutes to get off this lease."

"We're sticking with Tom," Norton said. "We fig-ure——"

McBride swerved the gun abruptly and let loose a shot between them. Then, as they fell back, he swung the gun back on Lord.

"You're my prisoner," he said. "I'm making a citizen's arrest."

"You can do that," Lord said. "Don't make much sense, though."

"Trespassing!" said McBride. "Willful destruction of property!" His voice rose. "Breaking and entering!" Now yelling. "Larceny!"—screaming.

The screaming continued through a jumbled, run-to-gether, incoherent mass of accusations. And then, abruptly, he began to giggle. This went on for a full minute, then ended as suddenly as the screaming had.

"You there," he said, jerking his head at Joyce. "Get that piece of rope and tie your boy friend's hands behind him."

Joyce smirked nervously, either unable or unwilling to follow the command. Lord caught her eye, silently indicated that she was to obey. But still she could not or would not.

McBride eyed her terribly, the cords in his throat swelling. "Do you hear me, you whore? Do as I tell you!"

"W-*Whore?*" Joyce suddenly came to life. "You calling me a whore, mister?"

"Yes, whore!" McBride seemed to delight in the word. "The lowest kind of whore! A filthy, slimy whore! A cheap, stinking, rotten——"

She was not an unduly sensitive person, except where her own feelings were concerned. Neither was she inclined to look ahead to the potential consequences of her acts. This character had called her a whore. She didn't take that kind of talk from anyone; period; end of story.

She was gripping her purse in her right hand. Without a word, in one furious unbroken motion, she drew her arm back, swung, and let go. The heavy bag zipped toward him, trailing a tinkling stream of cosmetics, bobby pins, and small change. Instinctively, he threw up his arms to ward it off.

In the next instant, Lord hit him with a flying tackle. McBride dropped like a rock, but he held onto the gun. He and the deputy went rolling and sprawling among the weeds. They came to their feet, and were as quickly down again, scrambled together in a struggling, tangled mass of flailing feet and slugging fists. It was impossible to intervene, but Joyce moved closer, eyes still blazing with offended dignity, and the two oil-field workers stood poised alertly, ready to leap into the fray at the slightest opportunity.

Then, the gun began to explode, and the three scampered

backward. They were still running, heads ducked, bodies crouched, when there was a final shot, dully muffled this time.

And then there was silence.

McBride lay spread-eagled on his back, his outflung right hand still gripping the gun. Lord was slowly rising from his body, staring down at him. Then, jerkily pulling his gaze away, he brushed his mouth with the back of his hand. Dully he watched the approach of Joyce and his two friends.

Joyce was the first to reach the body. She took a quick glance at it, then spoke, half-defiantly, a small sob in her throat. "He shouldn't have done that. H-He had no right to call me a whore."

"He sure shouldn't have," Lord agreed. "He sure didn't."

"We shouldn't have come here in the first place! I told you we shouldn't! I begged and pleaded and—and——"

She began to weep, childlike, hands hanging at her sides, great glossy tears squeezing from her squinted-shut eyes. Lord took her by the shoulders and gently helped her into the car. Forcing a reassuring smile, he dabbed at her tears with a polka-dot bandanna.

"Better now, honey? Want to honk the old schnozzle?" He held the handkerchief while she blew into it. "What about old Tom gettin' you a drink of water?"

"I—I g-guess not. I'll j-just"—She got a look at herself in the car mirror—"oh, my God! Just look at me! Now, where is my——"

"You just sit tight. I'll get it for you."

He gathered up the contents of her purse, making sure that nothing was left behind. She grabbed the compact from him and went to work with it almost feverishly. Tom's mouth twisted as he turned away. She called to him sharply.

"Now, where do you think you're going? Let's get out of here!"

"We will. Got a little talkin' to do first."

"What's there to talk about? He's dead isn't he?"

"I reckon. Be pretty hard to live with no brains in his head."

She made a disgusted, sickish sound. Curly and Red looked up from the body as he approached them, then moved away at an angle as he nodded his head, joining him as he went up a gentle rise in the land and paused, back turned, at the crest.

"Didn't want to look at him no more," he explained. "Just didn't feel like I could take it."

They murmured sympathetically. Red asked him how it had happened.

"I don't rightly know; everything happened so fast. Of course, I was trying to get the gun away from, but I don't think I had a hold of it when he got killed. Just seemed like he flung it against his head and pulled the trigger."

"It wasn't your blame, Tom."

"Well, it sure wasn't intentional. But it wouldn't have happened if I hadn't been here."

"You got no call to blame yourself," Curly insisted, "an'

nobody can fault you for it. Any trouble about it, you got us and the lady to tell what happened."

"You think about that for a minute," Lord said. "See if you can't find just a leetle somethin' wrong with the picture."

He rubbed his eyes tiredly, looked down the slope among a stand of blackjack trees. Several oblongs of natural rock had been laid there, abutting to form a building foundation. Affixed to them were the edge-up timbers of the studding.

"McBride's house," Norton answered his silent question. "He was bringin' his wife out here as soon as she had her baby. Wanted to have 'em a good long way from town, I reckon."

"I thought his wife was dead."

"This is his second one. Used to be what you'd call his ward, I guess." Norton grinned feebly. "One way of gettin' a wife. Raise her yourself."

Lord looked down at the ground. Curly frowned at Red.

"About what you was sayin' a minute ago, Tom. What . . . ?"

"Well, suppose the killin' had been my fault. You're my friends, and you didn't have no use for McBride. What would your story have been?"

"Well . . ." said Curly. "Oh, yeah, I see what you mean."

"You're sayin'," said Norton, "that our word don't amount to nothin'?" He frowned, scratched his head uneasily. "Come to think about it, I guess it don't either."

"Oh, it amounts to something, all right. If you said this

was all my fault, folks'd believe you right off. It's only if you back me up that they won't."

"What do you want to do, Tom?"

"Well, that kinda depends on you boys. Don't want you puttin' your tail in a sling for me, but . . ."

He explained his plan. The two men were agreeing to it long before he had finished. He was not asking them to perjure themselves; only to say nothing unless he later told them to. And that seemed safe enough. They had been fired along with the other workmen on the well. Like the others, they *could* have left soon after the firing; they could have no knowledge of McBride's death or, of course, of Lord's presence at the well. Some one would be stopping by the lease tomorrow; some supply man or mud-washer [*geologist*] or company scout. Let him discover the body, and report it.

Red and Curley were both confident that the scheme would work. Lord was not so sure, but conceded that the death did look like suicide.

"And it kind of was in a way," he added dully. "Might be it really was."

They walked back down the hill with him. They shook hands. As he drove off, they were hastily repairing the tool-house door and disposing of the other mementos of his visit.

With the approach of sunset, the August evening had turned cool. And as the sun dropped abruptly below the horizon, the cool became cold. Lord put up the car top and closed the windows. Then, moodily, he drove on again.

He had hardly spoken since leaving the lease. Now, as Joyce began to prod him insistently, he told her of his talk with Red and Curly and about what they had agreed.

She started to nod. Then, instead, her eyes narrowing slightly, she withdrew to her own side of the seat and sat there, looking straight ahead, a strange primness modifying the lines of her hard-pretty face. Lord gave her a quickly covert look. Grinning sadly to himself, he fumbled for a cigar, found none, and dug a wooden match from his pocket. He tucked it into the corner of his mouth and began to chew on it.

" 'Course, I didn't ask how you felt about it," he observed. "Didn't figure I had to. Just thought you'd go along with whatever I said."

"We-el, I'd certainly *like* to, Tom. You know I'm always anxious to do whatever you want."

"Uh-huh?"

"I—I'm not what I used to be, Tom. I haven't been since we started going together."

"So I noticed," Lord said. "Been wonderin' how you got by fi-nan-shelly."

"Well, I haven't been really. I've had to do without a lot. But I haven't minded. I'd do anything for you, Tom; anything! But maybe—well, you know—a girl like me, a girl that's been what I've been . . ."

Lord's grin became open. He gave her a jovial slap on the thigh. "Now, why don't you just come right out and say it? Shouldn't be so hard. Might choke on it, if you hold it in any longer."

"Well." Joyce took a deep breath, bracing herself. "We'd better get married, Tom. A woman can't testify against her own husband."

Lord nodded; he said idly, "There's something else a woman can't do."

"Yes?"

"She can't testify if she's dead."

5

Aaron McBride's second wife, Donna, was the oldest of fourteen children, five of whom were still alive. At the age of fifty, her mother became pregnant with the fifteenth child, and died during its gestation. Her father promptly abandoned the family and went on about his career of True Gospel preaching. The younger children were taken into an orphanage. Being old enough to be "useful," as well as a distant relative of McBride's wife, Donna found refuge in his household.

Donna earned her keep, and then some. She was only thirteen at the time, but she had been doing a woman's work for years—assuming a woman's responsibilities except the marital ones. Mrs. McBride firmly encouraged her to continue doing the first, and gradually allowed her to take over the second.

Mrs. McBride's health was poor; she had little interest in pleasing her husband. She could not say why—not *exactly* why—she felt as she did about him. He was a good provider, and an unswervingly faithful and undemanding husband. Most of the time he was away in the fields, while she lived comfortably, almost luxuriously, in Fort Worth. Still, she could barely tolerate him. She dreaded his visits home, and was always glad to see him leave. And Aaron McBride knew it.

He had had no home, in the true meaning of the word, until Donna's coming. She gave him one. While Mrs. McBride, after allowing her cheek to be kissed and a few polite formalities, withdrew to her bedroom, Donna saw to his needs—fixing his meals, taking care of his laundry, talking to him, and encouraging him to talk as long as he wished: doing everything she could to make him feel welcome and wanted.

She was grateful for the opportunity to do things for him. It seemed to her that she could never do enough. He was the father she had never had—the strong, wise, and good friend who could have been no more interested in her welfare if she had been his own daughter.

At his expense she received extensive medical and dental treatment. At his expense her near-illiteracy was overcome; she was cram-tutored, made able to enter high school only a year or so behind her age group. She worked hard around the house, but he would not allow her to become a drudge. She was to have ample time for her studies, and time and money for at least a few of the pleasures that other girls enjoyed. And he was unusually firm with his wife when she showed resentment at his "coddling," or attempted to oppose his wishes.

So Donna's affection for the man, her gratitude to him,

were completely in order. She did not see how she could ever do enough to repay the debt she owed him.

When, following his wife's death, a means of repayment seemed open to her, she almost snatched at the opportunity.

Love? Did she love him? Well, of course, she did! How could she help herself, and who else would she love if not him? He was twenty-five years older than she, but that made no difference. He was young enough for her, and she was old enough for him.

After their marriage and a brief honeymoon in Fort Worth, he returned to the oil fields. She planned to join him as soon as he could find suitable living quarters and was sure of remaining in one place for a time. But even as she prepared to leave the Fort resident, he advised her to remain there. He did not explain why. She did not ask. He would have his reasons; when he was ready, he would tell her what they were, and she was content to wait until he did.

A scrupulously honest man, by his own code, he intended to tell her about the beating and what it had done to him, inwardly. She was his wife; she had a right to know. And he hungered for her sympathy, her asurance that he was right—that what he had lived by was right, and that Lord was wrong. But he was too reserved to make a direct appeal to her, and, at any rate, he could not find the right words. It was a simple thing, seemingly: he had had a fight as a result of a business misunderstanding. But it was all mixed up in his mind, and he could not talk about it. Lord had confused him as badly as he had beaten him.

On one of his quick visits home, he did approach the subject obliquely, attempting by means of a hypothesis, in which he was determinedly fair to the deputy, to get her opinion as to his rightness and Lord's wrongness:

Lord, he told her, was doubtless a good man at heart. Everyone spoke well of him, and he deserved much more than life had given him. On the other hand—well, wasn't his life his own lookout? Was anyone obligated to look out for his interests, to their own disadvantage perhaps, if he could not do so himself?

"Well"—Donna pondered the problem seriously, her forehead puckering in thought—"well, no, I suppose not. Like Pa used to say, it's everyone for himself in this world. But," she added, her face brightening as though the sun had risen behind it, "I'm awfully glad you don't feel that way. I'd hate to think where I'd be if you did."

McBride said uncomfortably that the two situations were different. He'd had a duty toward her, she being a child and his wife's relative.

"You did not! You just did it because you're you, and you'd be just as kind and considerate with Mr. Lord or anyone else." She hesitated, noticing the flicker of pain in his expression. "You—you do like Mr. Lord, don't you? I remember your writing me that he'd been very friendly to you."

"And he was! He has been!" Seeing the concern in her eyes, he hurried on hastily, making his voice firm and hearty. "Lord's been very friendly to me. No one could have been pleasanter than he has. I can't say that we see eye to eye on everything, but——"

"Yes, dear?" She had not noticed his use of the past tense. "But you do like him? You get along well together?"

"Now, why shouldn't we, child? He's a good man, and you know I'd never willfully offend anyone."

"Yes, I know. I just thought that, perhaps——"

"I'll tell you, Donna," McBride said, uncomfortable with his indirect lies and yet forced to tell another. "I think I'd trust Lord with everything I have, even if I didn't like him personally. If such a thing is possible, he's actually too honest."

"I'm so glad," Donna murmured. "You need a good friend like that."

It was the last time they talked about Tom Lord. McBride wanted to tell her the truth, but he did not know how to begin. He was too fearful of hurting her, or worrying her, or belittling himself in her eyes.

And, so, finally, before he could inform her that Lord was by no means his good friend, death came for Aaron McBride.

With the morning baths out of the way, and her fourth cup of coffee warming the flesh beneath her stiffly starched uniform, the nurse went down the corridor to 4-B (Surgical), hesitated before the threshold a moment as though to gather her strength, and cautiously opened the door. She was an older woman; gray-haired, crisp-voiced, authoritative of manner. She was used to fussy and demanding patients, and she knew just how to handle them. Yet she had delayed far longer than she should in calling on 4-B. For 4-B somehow made her nervous. The patient not only failed to grasp the idea that the nurses knew what was best for her, and that she should do as they told her, but clung to a directly opposite viewpoint.

Fortunately, the nurse saw with a sigh of relief, 4-B had fallen asleep. (After running everyone ragged for the past three days!) And cautiously crossing to the bed, she pulled back the patient's sheet. The short surgical gown had crawled upward, and the shaved crotch and abdomen, with their cruel Caesarean wounds, were fully exposed. The nurse glanced at them quickly; assuring herself, without much conviction, that the bandage-change could well wait a while.

She was still hesitating over her decision when the patient made it for her. Firmly grasping the sheet with both hands and pulling it back over her body, she said, "That can wait. Right now, I want you to bring me a telephone."

Oh, you do, do you? the nurse thought indignantly. *Well, just try and get it, you little snip!* And she said nervously, "Why, of course, dear. Did we sleep well last night? Have our bowels moved this morning?"

"Speaking for myself," said the patient, "the answer is yes to both questions. Now, you will please bring me a telephone."

"But, dear. You've already talked a number of times, and

it hasn't accomplished a thing. It just upsets you, and——"

"Perhaps. And I intend to do some upsetting myself, until something is accomplished."

The nurse looked down at her helplessly, her sense of being put upon slowly giving way, fading before a wave of tenderness and sympathy. Why, she was just a child really, this girl with the wide-set, wisely innocent eyes, the small, too-firm mouth. She might act like a woman, have more than her fair share of lush womanhood's characteristics, but she was still a child, in years and in experience. And in her direct approach, her complete unsubtlety of manner, the child in her was constantly apparent.

"You poor, poor dear, you," the nurse said warmly. "I want you to know how sorry we all feel for you."

"I don't want you to feel sorry for me. I want a telephone."

"To lose your husband and your baby in less than a week—a girl of your age! But . . . but we must accept these things, don't you see, dear? We must reconcile ourselves to them. If God, in His wisdom, sees fit to take our loved ones——"

"God in His wisdom did not see fit to do anything of the kind. Someone else is responsible, and I intend to find out who. And when I do, that someone is going to be sorry. So," said Donna McBride, half-rising in the bed, "either you get me a telephone right this minute, or by golly I'll get one myself!"

The nurse argued no more. A little wildly, moving at her fastest clip in years, she ran to get a telephone.

6

The house nestled behind a stand of blackjack on the edge of Big Sands, a neat blue-and-white cottage, with a lean-to at the rear for a garage, and a white picket fence surrounding its ample grounds. Drought-resistant ivy vines clustered around the windows and spread spiny fingers over roof and eaves. A crumbling sandstone walk, its interstices laced with hardy Bermuda grass, stretched from the gate to the front stoop.

Originally a parsonage, it had remained miraculously untouched by a cyclone which had lifted the adjoining church intact and scattered the pieces over a hundred miles of wasteland. The church was rebuilt in a closer-in and (its congregation hoped) a luckier location. The parsonage remained where it was; unoccupied, shied away from by potential tenants, lest they attract the fate which the original residents had escaped.

With the coming of the oil boom, of course, and the consequent housing shortage, the place was readily rented.

But the tenants came and went, moving in and out after a few weeks or a few months—moving farther out as the fields expanded, or moving on to oilier pastures. And in the opinion of the bank—the owner of the house—they were more trouble than they were worth. The constant necessity to clean up and refurbish for incoming tenants, to replace broken windows and rehang unhinged doors and repair the other wreckage which the oil-field crowd invariably left behind them, practically absorbed the rent they paid, inflated as the rent was. A permanent tenant was needed—someone who, being permanent, would be concerned with keeping the place livable.

Joyce Lakewood became that tenant.

Her landlord, naturally, did nothing so discourteous as to inquire into her source of income. Perhaps, in such un-civilized areas as Dallas, Fort Worth, and Houston, the question—with all its ugly implications—would have been raised, but it was not done out here. The lady was obviously a responsible person. What her business was, and her banker-landlord could pretty well guess what it was, was her own business.

Every town needed at least one "fancy lady." The need was as obvious as it was for gambling joints and bootleg-gers. It was the obligation of the law not to prohibit them, but to see that they were properly regulated.

So Joyce settled down in Big Sands in the one-time par-sonage of the church, and except for the bluest-nosed of its populace—fanatics, in the town's opinion—no one objected. The law, in the person of Tom Lord, did visit her. But this was merely routine. It was only doing what was expected of it, fulfilling its unwritten obligations.

Lord was elaborately polite. But he was still a cop; and cops, to her way of thinking, were all alike. They either had their hand extended or drawn back, ready to slug you or take something from you. And a lot of times they did both.

So Joyce too was polite, but barely so; the minimum necessary to skirt trouble. She answered his questions promptly, but coldly.

No, she had never been convicted or even arrested on a felony charge. For misdemeanors, yes: vagrancy, consorting, soliciting, and the like. But nothing serious. Yes, she was aware that her record could be checked. He was welcome to check hers; in fact, it would suit her just fine if he did.

Yes, her health was excellent, and she intended to keep it that way. A girl should do that for her own sake, even if she didn't have any respect for other people.

He was finished very quickly; with the formal questioning, that is. But still he lingered, studying her, his eyes shrewdly humorous beneath their delicately arched brows.

"Reckon you didn't like this much," he said. "Don't exactly cotton to it myself."

"It's all right. I'm used to it."

"Yeah? Don't see how you hardly could be." He pushed himself up from his chair, announced that he'd better be getting along. "You suppose I could see you again some time?"

"What's to stop you?" Joyce shrugged. "Any time, on the house."

Lord looked at her sharply. Then, with a curtly courteous nod, he left the house.

She did not see where she had blundered, but she knew that she had, and she knew that getting a cop down on you was very bad business. Thus, after an apprehensive three days, she was eagerly pleasant when he called her.

"Why, of course, it's all right, Mr. Lord. It's not short notice, at all. I'll be expecting you, so come right on in."

Lord said maybe it would be better if she just came right on out. "Be dinnertime, after we get down a drink or two, and I'm kinda hungry."

"Din—But I thought that—that—" She got a grip on herself. "All right, Mr. Lord. I think I'm kinda hungry myself."

She supposed that, after dinner and drinks in the town's spanking new hotel, she would shortly find herself in one of its bedrooms. But Lord merely took her for a drive in the country and then returned her to her doorstep, circumspectly declining her invitation to come inside.

"Kinda late, you know, an' people talk a lot in a small town."

He tipped his hat and departed, leaving her completely bewildered and warmed by an emotion she had never felt before. In the ensuing weeks, they were together almost every day.

He cooked dinner for them at his house, a very good dinner eaten to the accompaniment of hi-fi operatic recordings. They had picnics in the country. They went on long drives to the town's far-flung neighbors. Always, whatever they did or wherever they went, Lord was the essence of correctness. After a time, he did kiss her and embrace her, but never in the manner she was accustomed to. There was as much giving in it, as taking. He was sharing something, not brutally depriving her.

Once, falteringly, she inquired into his nominal aloofness: was it, perhaps, rooted in some organic difficulty? Lord laughed tenderly at the question.

"Nothin' like it, honey. Maybe I'll prove it to you before long. Meanwhile, well, I figure that somethin' you get for nothin', or next to nothin', is just about worth that. Aside from that . . ."

"Yes, Tom?"

"I figured you needed somethin'—somethin' you'd never had before, or had too far back to remember—and I figured it would do me good to give it to you."

When, at last, there was the ultimate coming together between them, it was a completely new experience for her. It was as though it was the first time, instead of one of a near-endless series. She felt like a bride; like a person died and brought to life again.

And strangely, once the immediate ecstasy was over, she was unhappy. Dissatisfied. What he had given her he could as readily take away. And she could not allow that; the thought of it was unbearable.

She had to be sure of him, to have him bound to her; and if that could be done—and, of course, it could not, really—there was only one way to do it.

She began to hint at it. Lord was impervious to the hints. She asked for it openly, and he blandly evaded the request. She begged, nagged, and threatened. Lord's attitude was correspondingly sympathetic, sarcastic, and blunt.

She tried to remember this: that Lord invariably reacted, in kind, to her actions. He would treat her as well—or better—as he was treated, and he would hit back as hard—or harder—as he was hit. But wanting what she did, wanting it so badly, she could not be fair to him. Not until tonight, this night of McBride's death, could she admit that she had probably pressed her quest too hard.

"Tom," she said, as he stopped the car in front of her house. "I didn't mean what you thought I did—what it sounded like. I'd never do anything to hurt you."

"Well, that's fine," Lord said. "Reckon we both got nothin' to worry about then."

"Aren't you—won't you come in? It won't be any trouble at all to fix dinner for you."

"Reckon not," Lord said. "Ain't really hungry right now."

She looked at him anxiously, timidly laid a hand on his arm. "Then, come back later. Please, Tom! I—I don't want you to feel like you must. I can't stand it, darling! Please promise me you'll come back."

Lord fumbled at his shirt pocket, frowned, and drummed nervously on the steering wheel. He drawled that if he didn't get a see-gar pretty soon, he was goin' plumb out of his mind.

"Let me get you one, Tom! There's almost a whole box in the house. I——"

She reached for the car door eagerly. He gestured, restraining her.

"Somethin' I got to do," he said. "Don't know just how long it'll take, and I might not be real good company afterward. But if you really want me to come back . . ."

"Oh, I do, darling! I do!" She kissed him warmly, again moved toward the door. "And, Tom, honey, would you put your car around in back, please? I imagine you'll be staying quite a while—I hope you will, anyway—and it doesn't look very nice to leave it parked out in front."

Lord agreed, sober-faced, silently laughing with wry wonderment. Then he helped her out of the car and drove off.

Originally, the town had consisted of little more than a courthouse, standing at the end of a dusty main street whose largest building was a false-front store—groceries & meats, ladies' & gents' ready-to-wear, hardware, furniture and undertaking—and whose one place of amusement was a pool hall. Now, with the oil boom, Main Street was almost a mile long, and it boasted a fourteen-story hotel and a handsome sandstone-and-granite bank building. But in most respects the basic character of the town remained peculiarly unchanged. Only the oldest structures, the shabby nucleus of the place, seemed to have any permanence. There was a wraithlike quality about the others, the hastily thrown-up shops, honky-tonks, gin mills, and cothouses—yes, even the magnificient hotel and bank—an air of restless hovering, as though they had been brought here by the wind and must inevitably move on with it.

Sadly, although why he was sad about it he wasn't sure, Lord pictured the town as it once was and knew, with prophetic certainty, that it would be that way again. In a few years; a few decades, at most. It was only a matter of time until the magic of oil would lose its potency, and the town would be as it had been. Just another wide place in the road. Just big sands.

Years ago, over in the wilderness of Iraan-way, he had waded a shallow place in the Pecos, and plowing through the tangled brush and trees on the other side, had come into a city. Its central square was paved. Its business structures were solidly and expensively built. In the tiled lobby of the motion picture theater stood a beautifully sculpted fountain—dry now, nested with scorpions and centipedes. For there was no one in the city. There had been no one there for so long that few people in Iraan knew of its existence and none could even remember its name.

Lord drove slowly down the Main Street of Big Sands, expertly weaving a path between the high-booted men with their mud-daubed hats and the huge twenty-two-wheel trucks. He drove slowly, his manner idly deceptive, eyes and ears alerted for trouble in the raucous chaos of swarming crowds, coin pianos, and tinkling glassware.

The city and county fathers had never been of a mind to banish the boom's illegal elements; only to control them.

For "everyone," as was generally known, liked to drink, just as "everyone" liked to gamble and whore around a little. And as long as a man hurt no one but himself, what difference did it make?

Tom Lord guessed that it made no difference to him, if it made none to others. He guessed it was every man's right to make a damned fool of himself. *"Sic transit gloria,"* he thought, parking his car at the courthouse curb. "Eat, drink and be merry, for tomorrow . . ."

He got out of the car and entered the courthouse.

He climbed the stairs to the second floor and went down the shadowy, linoleum-floored corridor to the sheriff's office. There was a light on there. He paused on the threshold, pushing the Stetson back from his forehead.

"Somethin' I got to tell you," he said. "Didn't know whether I should at first, but I guess I better. I just killed a fella . . ."

7

Sheriff Dave Bradley had changed radically since the pre-boom days of Big Sands. Or, to be fair, time and circumstances had changed him. Insofar as he was conscious of change, he disliked it and fought against it. He hated the increased responsibilities of his job, the necessity to be an important executive instead of a simple lawman. He hated the advancing age which made him curt without cause, peevish and suspicious without reason. Yet he could not hold back the years, and he would not retire from office.

Sometimes he would hint at retiring, suggest that he was too old for the job and that a younger man was needed. But his friends and subordinates knew better than to agree with him. Or, if they didn't, they soon learned. He wanted assurance, not agreement. He wanted to be told that he wasn't old, that he was more than capable of his duties. So that was what he was told.

He continued to run for office. Since no one would think of opposing him, he continued to be elected. Why not, anyway? Where was the harm? It made old Dave feel good, and Tom could do his work for him. Tom'd been doin' it for years, and a few more wouldn't hurt none.

Dave Bradley heard this talk—that Lord, not he, was the real sheriff. He was successively hurt, angry, and suspicious, and he reacted accordingly.

He would give Lord an order, then curtly ask why he was carrying it out or accuse him of doing it in a way contrary to his instructions. Tom was gettin' pretty big for his britches, wasn't he? Kinda tossing his weight around. Well, maybe he'd just better do what he was told, and nothin' else but.

Sometimes—as today, for example—he would literally shoo Lord from his office, dismiss him from his day's duties. Never mind about the piled-up work. He knew how much work there was, and he didn't need no help from smart-alecks. All he asked was that Lord keep out of his way, do his loafin' and playin' around somewheres else.

Lord took the abuse quietly. He knew what lay behind it, and he felt indebted for past favors to Bradley. Yet taking it, he didn't like it. He himself had problems. In a sense, he had the same problem that Dave had: age. He was rushing toward the same void that the old man shrank back from. And Dave couldn't see that. He would make no allowances. Like most people who demand and expect understanding, he had little to give.

And tonight was one time when Lord had to have it.

"I mean it, Dave," he said slowly, for Bradley seemed not to have heard his opening statement. "I killed Aaron McBride."

Dave said with absent querulousness that that was no excuse. No excuse at all for Tom's slacking off all day. "Had to kill him, you ought to of done it on your own time. County's payin' you a plen-tee good salary to——— *Aaron McBride!*" he croaked, his mouth dropping open. "Why for did you do that?"

"I couldn't help it. For that matter, I ain't real sure he didn't kill himself," Lord said, and he explained what had happened. "O' course, it wouldn't have happened if I hadn't been there on the lease. But———"

"But you couldn't leave him alone, could you? You was just spilin' for trouble with him! Couldn't find an excuse, so you made one!"

"Now, that ain't so, Dave," Lord began, and then his voice trailed off into silence. *But wasn't it so? Hadn't he broken that spring deliberately?*

"Well?" Dave leaped on the silence venomously. "That's what happened, ain't it?"

"Maybe," said Lord slowly. "Maybe and maybe not. I didn't think it was that way, but it could've been."

"And now he's dead. Should've been here in the office workin', but you had to go wanderin' off and kill him."

"Look, Dave!" Lord said sharply. "Don't keep"—he broke off with an effort; shrugged tiredly—"yes, and now he's dead."

Bradley scowled at him, his mouth working irritably. "Ain't you got a lick of sense, Tom? You think that beatin' a man up and killin' him is the same thing?"

Lord shook his head curtly. He was aware, he said, that

there was plenty of difference. "They wouldn't hold still for murder, even if they didn't like McBride."

"You just bet they wouldn't! Probably venue you out of the county, so's the charge'd be sure to stick. Dammit Tom," Bradley threatened, "you just hadn't ought to've done it! Don't make no never-mind how many witnesses you got. Just one of 'em switches his story an' says it was your fault, you're stuck."

Lord hesitated. He said, finally, "None of 'em are going to switch. No one needs to know I was anywheres near McBride."

"Huh—how you mean?"

Lord told him. Bradley looked relieved for a moment, and then his face began to darken.

"You put me on a spot, Tom. Got my duty t'do, and you just about make it impossible."

"Wh-aat?" Lord stared at him bewilderedly; and then, comprehension darkening his eyes. "Do you really think that, Dave? That I told you this to tie your hands? You don't think I was just trying to be fair and honest with you?"

Bradley glowered at him. Peevishly, he skirted the question. "Been gettin' mean for a long time, Tom. I seen it coming on, an' I warned you about it, an' it didn't do no good. Wouldn't listen to me; thought you knew more'n I did. Now——"

"Now, I accidentally killed a man; maybe killed him. An' if you want to see me hung for it, here I am."

He extended his wrists. Bradley snorted, slapped at them angrily.

"That's the trouble with you, Tom," he complained. "Won't listen to no one. Can't say a word to you no more."

"Think you said just about a-plenty," Lord said coldly, "an all t' once it's beginnin' to sink in on me. Can't keep my ears stoppered to it no more, so I reckon I better walk away from it."

He pushed himself up from his chair, plucking the badge from his shirt. He tossed it on the sheriff's desk, turned, and started for the door.

"Aw, Tom. Tom, boy. . . ." The old man came shakily to his feet. "You know me, Tom. I'm just so danged tired and worried I hardly know which end I'm on. I didn't mean that——"

Over his shoulder, Lord said tightly that *he* meant it. He'd had all he cared to take, and then some.

Bradley continued to protest feebly. Protesting, he trailed after the deputy for a few steps. Then, as Lord made no answer, firmly continuing on his way, the pleading stopped abruptly and his voice became shrill with outrage.

"All right, Tom Lord! Go ahead an' be stubborn! Be as ornery as you danged please. But I'm warnin' you. You just—*you better listen to me, Tom!*"

"Yes?" Lord paused outside the door. "I'm listening, Dave."

"You just get out of line a little, an' see what happens! Just let me hear one peep about McBride, an' see what happens! I won't cover up for you. I'll pull you in so fast, it'll make your head swim."

He went back to his desk, then, old Dave Bradley. He sat there, glowering and muttering to himself, his eyes slowly moistening, his withered mouth puckering. And, finally, he dropped his head into his hands and began to cry.

Meanwhile, up near the center of town, Tom Lord was emerging from a liquor store with two large bags full of whisky.

Back in his car, he popped the cork from one bottle and up-ended it into his mouth. He drank in great gulps, until the stuff burbled up out of his lips and ran down over his shirt. Then, he recorked the bottle, tossed it to a grinning group of curbside spectators, and sped off toward Joyce's house.

She heard him coming; heard his clattering attempts to open the front gate. Almost instantly, she was out of the house, pulling him out of the car and sliding behind the wheel herself.

"You go on inside now, honey. I'll—can you make it all right?"

Owlishly good-humored, Lord said that of course he could make it. He couldn't take it, but he could always make it. And walking very straight, he headed across the yard.

By the time Joyce had put the car away, locking the lean-to door behind, he was in the kitchen, ponderously opening one bottle after another.

"Oh, now, Tom!" She began to restopper the bottles. "Why, do you act like this, honey? If you want a drink or two, fine, but you—Tom, now stop it!"

He was uncorking the bottles again, taking a swig from each as he did so. She tried to stop him, and casually, his stiff-armed palm rocked her backward, sent her reeling and staggering across the room until the wall stopped her with a painful thud.

The impact knocked the wind out of her, left her sickishly dizzy for a moment. As she clutched a chairback for support, Lord left the bottles and gently helped her sit down.

"He shouldn't have done that," he said, frowning at the sink where he had so recently stood. "I don't think I like him."

"H-He?" Joyce gasped. "What do you mean, *he*?"

"Gone now," said Lord, with an expression of satisfaction. "Wouldn't've been here in the first place, 'cept for your interference. Not chiding you, y'understand. City girl wouldn't know about prairie fires."

He took a long drink from his glass, rolled it around in his mouth. He took another drink, nodded to her seriously.

"Have to backfire 'em, burn off ground in front of 'em. Got nothing to feed on, they burn out. You follow me, Miss?"

"Of course, Tom. I understand. Now——"

"Apply the same principle with cloudburst. Just substitute liquid f'r fire. Defense always corresponds t' the impending threat 'r' disaster. Fire against fire, liquid against

75

liquid, an'—an'——" He hiccuped, rubbed his eyes wearily. "Ver' complex problem. Not something you c'n reduce to ten words o' basic English. But you understand principle, Joyce?"

Joyce assured him warmly that she did understand. She was also sorry, she said, that she had so thoughtlessly interfered with him.

"You can have all you want to drink, dear. If there isn't enough here, I'll go out and get some more. Now, why don't we go into the living room where we can be comfortable."

"Now, it can be told, Joyce. The hidden secret 've the ages is about t'be revealed."

"Uh-huh. Certainly, Tom; and we'll just take the bottles into the living room with us."

She got him into the living room, seated him in an easy chair with a full bottle of whisky in his hand. Then, as he talked and drank, she knelt in front of him, gently loosened his shirt collar and his belt, and slid off the ridiculously small, handmade boots.

She had seen him, taken care of him, on only one other binge. That was the day when the lease swindle had become obvious and, in effect, undenied. He had been sodden that time, drunk for a solid week. But he had not acted as he did now, on this occasion. This one had really scared her out of her pants. For a few minutes it was as though she were dealing with some terrifying stranger, instead of her drawling, kidding Tom Lord.

Yet he seemed to be all right, now. No longer frightening,

at least, and much less a stranger. He wasn't making too much sense; still talking in that overserious way. But gradually the stranger was fading, blending with the old familiar Tom.

". . . I'll tell you somethin', Joyce. There is no open season on man, pop'lar opinion n' practice to the contrary notwithstandin', an' any violation of his person's an infringement of the natural law. You grasp that, Joyce? Ought t'be pretty simple f'r great thinker like you. Someone 'at knows what all the movie stars eat for breakfast."

"Aah, now, Tom," Joyce laughed tenderly. "I'm not that bad, am I?"

" 'S'smatter of semantics an' custom. Liable to vary from day t'day. Howsomever, there is certain eternal truths an' customs, one of which, despite many interruptions, I am about to propound. T-t-to wit: The Lord law of the disintegration o' farts in high winds."

Joyce laughed again, half-protestingly. Lord waggled a finger in a reproving manner.

"Think about it," he said. "Tragedy of the ages. Because nothin' and no one is ever completely destroyed; simply assumes new shapes 'n' forms. Take me now, f'r example. Ask you if I'm destroyed, 'n' the answer is yes an' no. Or no'n' yes, if you prefer. Know what I'm talking about. Speakin' from personal experience . . . I . . . I . . . ." His eyes clouded, and he looked around wildly. "Where is it? What did you do with the bot fire?'

"Here! Right here, honey!"

She thrust a fresh bottle into his hands.

He drank from it gaspingly, and his eyes cleared again. "Know what I'm talkin' about. Had the clouds dropped spang on me, like cow-dab on a flat rock, with a consequent removal o' the terrain from b'neath my well-shod feet. Can't just hang there, can I? Defies the law o' gravity. So I jump to 'nother piece of ground, an' I just get dug in good there when there's another cloudburst, and I have to jump again. An' then there's another one, an'—an'——" He scrubbed his face with one hand, slowly kneaded his forehead. "Used to tell us in school that where there was no ears to hear there was no sound. Same thing applies visually. Fact that folks can't see somethin' don't mean it ain't there, or if they don't see it like it is that it ain't. Fact that they don't see a car bearin' down on, don't mean they ain't gonna get hit. Just means they can't see good. B-bad"— he belched—"very bad, Joyce. You can't do that."

"Yes? Yes, honey?"

"Yes, what?"

"What is it that you can't do?"

"Pat your head and rub your stomach at the same time."

With that the stranger seemed to vanish completely, and he appeared to be himself again. Drunk, of course, but again her Tom.

Half-kidding, apparently more amused than disturbed, he told her of his interview with Bradley and his resignation as the latter's chief deputy.

"The old fool!" Joyce was loyally indignant. "But don't you feel bad about it, honey. You're better off out of that rotten job."

"Out of there t' where?" Lord asked, but Joyce didn't seem to hear him.

"We'll just pull out of here, that's what. Go to some real nice place like Florida or California."

"You mean I could pimp for you? Well, gee, lady, I ain't had no experience, but I'm sure strong an' willing to learn."

"Don't, Tom. Please don't talk like that . . ."

"Or you could pimp for me," Lord said. "I could be your he-whore." He elaborated on this prospect, his voice rising above her pleadings and protests. "Yes, sir, that might be all right. I could get me one of them permanent waves and maybe some black silk underwear, and you could get out an' hustle me. Hang around hotel lobbies durin' conventions, or maybe at high-class bars. You see a likely lookin' dame, an' you give her the proposition." He winked lewdly in demonstration, holding his hand to the side of his mouth. " 'How about a nice fella for the night, lady? I got a real hot brunette on the string that's just itchin' for action.' "

Joyce made her face angry, her involuntarily quirking mouth severe. She said he wasn't being a damned bit funny, and his drunkenness was no excuse for such talk. "I mean it, Tom. I'd do j-just about anything in the w-world for you. But—b-but——" She spluttered, gurgled, and, then, suddenly doubled with laughter. She rocked back and forth, still kneeling, weakly slapping the rug with her hands.

". . . so," Lord drawled on, fiendishly, "you bring her up t'my room, and I prance around with my hand on one hip, kinda jouncin' and flouncin', y' know, until her pants begin to smoke. An' then——"

"T-Tom, you—*ha, ha, ha, ha*—Tom, if y-you don't stop, I-I'll—*aaah, ha, ha, ha, ha*. . . ."

Lord grinned, mercifully subsided. He dropped down on the floor with her, and they clung together, laughing, kissing, and fondling each other. At last, they were very quiet, the only sound the beating of their own hearts and the rhythm of their own breathing and the distant *drip-drip* of the kitchen sink. Then, without taking her mouth from his, Joyce hooked the lamp cord with her foot, yanked, and unplugged it from the wall.

Lord didn't know how many drink-drugged days had passed when the squat, thick-set man with the cropped hair called on Joyce Lakewood. At the time, and even for some time afterward, he was not even sure that she had had such a visitor or any visitor. Everything was clear enough while it was taking place, but the clarity was dreamlike—a brilliant light flashed on in a dark room, then snapped off again, leaving a darkness that seemed never to have been penetrated.

It was at night, he believed, when he floated up out of a black abyss and came slowly into consciousness. Still inert, sprawled on his back, he watched with slitted eyes as Joyce pulled a robe over her body and silently opened the door of the room. She stood there a moment, pausing on the threshold while she studied him. Then, satisfied, certain that he was still knocked out, she went through the door and silently closed it again.

Lord stared at it intently; turning the knob, in his imagination, as she had done. He focused on it, all else blotted out of it, and the door came open. Only for an inch or two, but definitely open.

He remembered being very pleased with himself. He remembered telling himself that any accomplishment, regardless of its nominal impossibility, could be as readily achieved by concentration. That was all you had to do, just think and keep on thinking, and what you desired would be yours.

Now, why didn't I start doing this sooner? he thought. *I'll have to——*

He heard the voices then, Joyce grudgingly admitting the man at the front door. Without a sound, as though responding to an electric impulse, he came up off the bed, crossed the room, and peered out into the living room.

He was in the dark, and they were in the light, sitting conspiratorially—but by no means amiably—close together on the lounge. They were facing him, keeping an eye on the bedroom door, yet obviously unaware that it was slightly open. He could see them perfectly, even to the movement of their lips. But their voices were so low that he had to strain to hear them; could hear them clearly only at brief intervals.

"*. . . so how . . . I know? Knocked out anyway, isn't he?*"

"*. . . the hell you want?*"

"You know what we want. Just what we paid for."

". . . best I could. Every . . . I can with him."

". . . not enough. Not . . . with McBride . . . Don't mind him . . . but stink . . . lot of questions. . . ."

". . . think he did it?"

". . . reasons . . . Doesn't matter, anyway . . . pin him for it. . . . tough egg. Won't stop until. . . ."

". . . won't do it! I can't, damn you. I . . . ."

"Then, get him away from here, and . . . let him come back. Move him or pin him. Or we . . ."

His thick forefinger stabbed painfully into her breast. Joyce winced, biting her lip as she shrank back from him.

"Well? Think you got the idea?"

". . . got it."

"Hang onto it. It's the best one you'll ever have. . . ."

There were a few more words, all of them completely inaudible to Lord. They got up from the lounge, then, and Lord eased the door shut and lay down again.

He was back in his stupor almost as soon as he touched the bed.

8

George Carrington, president and general manager of the Highlands Oil & Gas Company (a Delaware Corporation; business offices, Fort Worth, Texas) lingered in the hospital corridor while the nurse went on into 4-B, carrying his gifts of a dozen long-stemmed roses and a five-pound box of candy. He was a tall, perfectly turned out man, quick of eye and smile, distinguished, and capable-looking. Yet, for all his air of confidence and capability, there was something wistful about him; a silent, pleading for understanding that was particularly attractive to women.

It was probably the one genuine thing about George Carrington, or at least, the most nearly. About a thousand per cent more genuine than say, his British mannerisms and speech. For Carrington did need understanding (to equate the term with sympathy). He stood constantly in need of it. He liked it and appreciated it, wherever it derived from. But he needed it most, to state an axiomatic paradox, from those who consistently withheld it from him. And since they did, his need—and his air of wistfulness—was constant.

The things truly important to George Carrington persistently went wrong for him. Even the relatively small things, the indirectly important.

Now, as the nurse emerged from 4-B, he saw that still another had gone wrong. With diffident apology, she extended the candy and flowers, holding them out to him yet also hanging onto them.

"I'm awfully sorry, Mr. Carrington. Mrs. McBride doesn't feel that . . . well, she doesn't want these."

"Really?" Carrington simultaneously managed a grave frown and a warm smile for the nurse. "Well, well, now. Perhaps later, eh?"

"I'm afraid not, sir. She doesn't want them at all. Shall I have them returned to your office, or . . . ?"

Carrington said that certainly she must not return them. She must, on the contrary, retain them for herself, and he would be deeply offended if she did not.

"You'll just convey my good wishes to our invalid, eh? A speedy recovery and all that. You do that for me, and I'll be more than repaid for these trifles."

"Why, I'll be glad to," the nurse beamed. "And thank you very, very much for——" She broke off, frowning. "But you'll see her yourself, won't you? I think you'd better, Mr. Carrington," she added, unwillingly firm. "I really think you'd better."

"But—but she's not feeling well! Can't be, you know. Obviously not at all fit, not at all herself."

"She's herself, all right," the nurse said grimly. "At least, I've never seen her any other way. Just about driven us crazy to get you out here, and now that you're here . . ."

She moved in front of him, blocking his way to the elevator. Carrington, with desperate dignity, unsuccessfully tried to move around her. Hands fluttering he fell back, declaring that he really didn't like this, you know. Didn't think it was at all wise to see Mrs. McBride at such a time.

"Love to, you know. Like nothing better. But must think of our invalid, eh?"

"That's who I am thinking of," the nurse said. "You go right on in, Mr. Carrington."

Carrington went in, perforce. And as always, when he was forced to do something, he did his best to make the most of it. He entered the door, not lingeringly, with feet dragging, but with quick eager strides. His smile was turned on to its fullest, and his eyes glowed with warmth, and he approached the woman in the bed with both hands extended.

"Dear Mrs. McBride! How nice of you to let me call! I've been wanting to get out for days, but . . ."

"Be quiet," said Donna McBride.

"Eh? Oh, now, really! Can't talk like that, can we? Old friends together, and——"

He stopped talking; sat down, with a silent philosophical sigh, in the chair she pointed to. For he'd done his best, hadn't he, and how could a chap do more than that?

For the next fifteen minutes, he remained in the chair, eyes bent attentively on Donna, nodding and shaking his head sympathetically, murmuring meaningless nothings as he seemingly drank in each word she said. Actually, he heard very little, his mind catching at only the most significant peaks of her talk. Actually, his absorption was not with her, but with himself. He was wondering how such a fine chap as he had become so hopelessly involved with such dreadful people.

Not Donna or her husband. McBride had been a terribly decent fellow; rather a bore, you know, but truly decent, and naturally she would hate to lose him. But the others, those responsible for the indubitable runaround she was getting—well! Really grim, you know. Oh, but grim! And being a fair-minded laddie, he could only blame himself for his entanglement with them.

"Should have spotted them, right off," he thought wearily. *"Should have known my luck was sour when the old witch bagged me."*

The old witch referred to was his dead wife, the widow of a Texas cattle millionaire. Carrington had met her in his job as shoe clerk in a fashionable Dallas store. Up until that time, or so he thought in retrospect, life had been very good to him.

He did a bit of photographic modeling, at quite attractive rates. The better-type women's stores were eager for his services, knowing that he either had a following or would very soon have one, and they paid well for them. Then, along with his direct earnings, there were innumerable gifts. Cash, quite often—a few bills slipped unobtrusively into his pocket, or under his dinner plate. If not cash, jewelry, heavy gold items that could be readily negotiated for cash. And once he had gotten a gift certificate for a complete wardrobe.

Of course, there could be some pretty tiresome encumbrances to these gifts. The donors were not the young juicy types which George Carrington would have preferred to show around in public and lie doggo with in private. Rather, since the young juicy types either had no money or saw no reason to spend it for male companionship, Carrington's bounty came from the definitely nonyoung and unjuicy. Not in their dotage, you know; still went in for a bit of guzzling, heel-kicking, and hanky-panky. But whether lean or fat, and they always seemed to be one or the other, their attractions did not include youth or juice.

Still, that was all right, wasn't it? A fellow couldn't have everything, now, could he? Particularly when the fellow in question was no longer quite so young himself, and whose depletion in juice was manifesting itself in an occasional twinge and increasing tiredness. On the contrary, such a chap should be thinking less about fun and more about the future. For if the last was taken care of, the first must follow as night does the day.

Thinking that way, and he was thinking that way more and more of the time, George was a sitting duck for the witch. She had him signed, sealed, and delivered to her lair before a lad could say knife.

He assumed naturally that he was entering a share-and-share-alike arrangement; each according to his need, and each according to his ability. The witch would toss her gilt into the connubial pot, and he would provide himself—jollying her by the hearthside during the long winter evenings, and bunting her about in the hay when the fever was upon her. Unfortunately, the witch had her own ideas about sharing.

"You're a real amusin' boy, Georgie," she told him, "and I get a kick out of showing you off. It's worth somethin' to me, and you're gonna get somethin'. A nice livin' free gratis, and enough income to let you hold your head up. What you ain't gettin' is wrote into my will. And you ain't gettin' a free ride. Won't ask much of you, 'cause you don't have it to put out. But you *are* takin' a job."

Like many people from old cattle families, the witch, as her dead husband had been, was contemptuous of oil ("stinkin' stuff," they thought of it) and the oil industry, and they would not directly or deliberately involve themselves with it. With their extensive holdings, however, it was inevitable that they should become indirectly involved—if only, as in the case of Highlands Oil & Gas, in the role of unwilling creditors. The widow owned Highlands, lock, stock and barrel. She didn't give a damn about it, and she was certain that it couldn't be worse off under George's management than it already was. So she turned it over to him.

George did his feeble best to make a go of it. He kept books, after a fashion. He kept the cubbyhole offices meticulously clean. Hunt and peck style, he typed out scads of letters, practically none of which needed to be written. In between these activities, he made frequent field trips. In those days, Aaron McBride constituted one-sixth of the company's working force. He was doubtless bewildered by President Carrington's "inspection tours" and "staff conferences," but George remembered him gratefully as being consistently respectful and always helpful.

Thanks largely to McBride, Highlands began to improve its position. It still lost money but not as much as it had, and the witch was hopeful eventually of cutting off the dole which it presently needed to survive.

Then, the widow died, and the dole ended with her life. George would receive a modest income from her estate. Highlands could either go under, or it could get by without assistance, and beloved husband George was welcome to it either way.

The witch was really rather unsporting, Carrington felt. Rather like endowing him with what the little boy shot at. Then, while he was considering junking the company, selling off its well-worn equipment for what it would bring, the grim chaps had appeared.

Not that they seemed grim at the time. Really quite jolly, as a matter of fact. They had heard a lot about George and Highlands, and they liked what they had heard, and they were ready to back their liking with money. George could have all he needed, within reason. If it went down the drain, okay; there was such a thing as a tax loss, and there would be no kicks. If it made money, that was okay, too. They'd divvy it up on some mutually satisfactory basis.

Now, they would want to recommend a good bookkeeper to him. George's time was obviously too valuable

to be spent at pencil pushing. Moreover, they would doubtless have helpful suggestions for George occasionally. But
the company was to be strictly his baby. He would be the
boss. He would remain the sole owner of record.

It seemed like a very nice arrangement to George; really
not half-bad. What it amounted to actually was that they'd
provide the money—toss it into the old fiscal pot, you
know—and he'd provide himself; and they'd all live happily ever after et cetera.

It occurred to him later that he had once before entered
a similar arrangement that had proved to be a snare and
delusion. But by then the trap was sprung. He was bagged,
even as the witch had bagged him. And compared with
them, his latest captors, the witch seemed quite jolly.

He could not walk out on them, as he had threatened
to with her. He could not get grim or haughty with them,
as he had with her. Oh, he *could*, but it didn't get him
anything. Nothing that a chap would exactly cherish, or
care to have repeated.

The most worrisome feature of the arrangement was the
fact that he seldom understood the import of the "suggestions" given him, and which he was required to pass on.
Nothing was ever explained to him. No one would tell him
why he should do this and why he should not do that. He
did know that McBride didn't like them. So he surmised
that putrid things were afoot. But the extent of their pu-
tridity, and how much else there might be that neither he
nor McBride had contact with . . .

He didn't know. By Jove, he just didn't know. He only

knew that he was in the midst of some pretty grim goings-on—McBride's death could be one of them—and that he, George Carrington, would be the ideal patsy if the old axe fell.

"Mr. Carrington! *Mr. Carrington . . . !*"

"What? Yes, my dear?" The glaze fled from George Carrington's eyes. "You were saying, Mrs. McBride?"

Donna stared at him steadily, her small jaw set. She looked him over, very carefully, a frown spreading over her face. Her anger and exasperation slowly dissolved, to be replaced by puzzlement.

"Mr. Carrington," she said, "do you really run Highlands Oil & Gas Company?"

Carrington had expected the question. He had seen that same look on the faces of others, and he had subsequently had the same question asked him. A rather unflattering question, when you stopped to think about it. But just how to answer it, at once plausibly and prudently, was something he had never figured out.

"Well, really," he laughed brightly. "President and general manager, you know. Says so right on the stationery."

"You seem to be pleasant and well-meaning, Mr. Carrington. I hoped you were just a figurehead. Otherwise, you must know why my husband's murder is being covered up."

"M-murder? Oh, now . . ."

"Murder. You haven't been listening, Mr. Carrington. I

couldn't get hold of you, and I couldn't get any satisfaction out of the Big Sands sheriff's office. So I hired a private detective." Donna paused for emphasis. "My husband's gun had been emptied, every bullet fired. And the slugs from them—excepting the one that killed him—were all within firing range of where he died."

Carrington looked blank. "Uh, well, now. Strange, isn't it? Mmm, yes. I see what you mean."

"Then, you know, he must have been murdered. He wouldn't have stood there firing aimlessly around the countryside and then put the last bullet in his brain."

Carrington shook his head wisely. He said it didn't seem likely, now, did it, yet one never knew, did one? "Very shrewd chaps, these detectives. Like to talk to a chap like that myself."

"Well, you won't be able to talk to this one. I got that one item of information from him; then he dropped the case. He came back here, closed his offices, and left town."

"Oh? Dashed peculiar, eh?"

"I'd say he was either scared off or bought off. Perhaps both. And I don't think you can help me find out why, can you, Mr. Carrington? It was a waste of time to have you come out here."

It was a simple statement of fact; not bitter, not rude. Yet Carrington found himself cringing, felt a hot flush of shame spreading over his pinkish, massaged face.

"Don't think I'd say that," he said rather stiffly. "Always willin', you know. Shoulder to the wheel, and all that sort of thing."

"Well . . . I suppose you could get me a gun."

"A—a gun? But——"

"But you won't, will you? Even that's too much for you. How did you manage to live this long, Mr. Carrington? Why did you want to?"

She turned on her side, turning her back to him.

Carrington grimaced with an attempt to smile. He tried to say something, to protest, to explain, but he could find nothing to say. He made another futile try, rising shakily, taking a half-step toward her bed. Then, his shoulders unaccustomedly squared, he pivoted and strode out of the room.

9

August Pinello's house was an old-fashioned, two-story brick in a good but by no means exclusive section of Fort Worth. It had a deep, wide lawn, with a croquet layout and a two-seat platform swing. August spent much time on the lawn; clipping the grass, sipping beer in the swing, or playing croquet. He was frequently joined in this last pastime by neighborhood children, who addressed him familiarly by his first name and whom he invariably stuffed with delicacies from his wife's kitchen.

Mrs. Pinello spoke little English, and she and her husband were seldom seen together except when they attended church. People guessed that he was probably a very lonely man. He owned a small string of service stations, but they seemed pretty well to run themselves. Now and then he had out-of-town visitors—simple, comfortable men like himself. But their stay was always brief, and August was soon alone on his lawn again.

Because of the visitors' coloring and other physical characteristics, it was generally assumed that they were his wife's relatives. For August's appearance held little hint of his heredity. His close-cropped hair was so blond that it seemed gray; and his massive neck flowed down into a body like a beer barrel. Built as he was, and with his huge red face and whitish hair, he looked to be sixty. Actually, he was twenty years younger.

About as slow-moving as a jet plane, that was the real August Pellino (alias Fat Gus Parkini, alias Augie the Hog). About as harmless and good-natured as a rattlesnake.

August liked children; there was no pretense about that. But if he had not liked them he would have seemed to; managed a thoroughly convincing masquerade. August always did whatever was necessary, and he did it well. His record for performance, regardless of its nature, was well-nigh perfect.

August was proud of his reputation, proud of his ability to obtain financing and well-heeled entrepreneurs for almost any scheme he cared to propose. But the responsibilities that went with such a reputation were always in the forefront of his mind, and he was always nagged by the prospect of failure.

He needed to have just one, only one, and the near-perfect record would be meaningless. Never mind the past. The past was past. The present was all that counted. As the instigator of an enterprise, August guaranteed its success. If his associates lost money on it, or were embarrassed or endangered by it, it was August's responsibility.

That was the inflexible code. He had enforced it with others, and he could not quarrel with it. But that made the ever-present threat no easier to bear. And when it began to gather substance, as it seemed to be now, when it came out of the hazy realm of potentiality and became an imminent possibility. . . .

With a sudden savage movement, August took a straight-down swing at a croquet ball, then grinned angrily as the ball split in half and the mallet handle broke in three places. He heard the slam of a car door, looked up. A cab was just wheeling away from the curb—*a goddamned circus wagon coming to his house!*—and George Carrington was moving purposely toward the gate.

Still grinning, a fat, hard hand extended, August walked toward him.

"Well, George," he said, taking firm possession of Carrington's hand, holding onto it as he urged him up the walk. "I guess I'm slipping in my old age. Didn't remember at all that I'd asked you to come out here."

"Oh? Uh, well you really didn't, Mr. Pellino. I——"

"Just decided to come on your own, huh? Well, that's just fine, George. We'll go right on in the house, someplace where it's nice and private, and have ourselves a little talk."

Carrington made a polite attempt to hang back. He said that he'd have to be rushing right off, and there was really no point to going inside. "It's about Mrs. McBride, Mr. Pellino. About her husband's murder, that is. I mean, she thinks it's murder."

"Murder? You mean suicide, don't you?"

"I—I'm afraid not," said Carrington, and he hastily babbled his reasons, Donna's reasons, why he did not.

"Think it's up to us to lend a hand, Mr. Pellino. Tab the killer for her, you know."

"But how could we do that, George? How would us businessmen know who the killer is?"

"Well, I—I just thought that, uh, perhaps——"

"Uh-huh. I think I know what you thought. I think you think too much, George. We'll have to have a nice long talk about it."

They had reached the steps leading up to the porch. Carrington made a frantic effort to break free. "Really must pop right off, old man. Can't even stay a mom—*aaah!*" His face went suddenly white with agony, and his knees half-buckled. Pellino gave him a yank, practically flung him up the steps to the porch.

"You could get your fingers broken that way," he grinned. "Might get them mashed right together, a man out of condition like you are."

"D-dont!" Carrington gasped. "Really shan't put up with this, you know. I—*aaah!*"

"That's your trouble, George. You think too much, and you don't get enough exercise. Let yourself get all run-down. Guess we'll have to take care of that, won't we?"

He yanked again, hurling Carrington into the dark hallway. Motioning for Carrington to precede him, shoving with his thick, bulging arms, he followed him down the hallway and into the kitchen.

A flour smudge on her nose, Mrs. Pellino was rolling out dough at a worktable. She looked up for a moment, glanced blankly at Carrington, and smiled incuriously at her husband. Then she went back to her work, and August pointed to a door on the far side of the room.

"Down there, George. And watch the stairs, huh? Get right on down them. Might fall if I crowd in on you."

"B-but, really. I——"

"Or maybe you don't mind falling? Well . . ."

He started lumberingly across the room. Carrington jerked the open door and went down the long, steep stairs. Above him the door closed, and the basement lights were turned on. Dully, he looked around.

Part of it was used as a wine cellar, lined with bottles in long, slanting bins. The rest formed a comfortably unpretentious recreation room. There was a small bar with three leather stools. There was a long leather divan, and four or five deep leather chairs.

Pellino gripped Carrington by the necktie, nodded toward the lounge. "Look all right, Georgie? Like to sit over there?" he said. And shifting his weight suddenly, he flipped Carrington over his shoulder and sent him flying across the room.

Carrington landed half-off, half-on the lounge, aching, stunned, the breath knocked out of him. Before he could rise, Pellino was on him again, again gripping him by the tie.

"Ain't very comfortable there, huh, George? Well, let's see. Suppose we try that chair over there."

His shoulders weaved again with the shifting of his weight. He stooped and jerked, and Carrington went hurtling through the air a second time. He came down, as he had before, half-on, half-off, the leather target.

He wasn't comfortable there either, of course. Pellino was sure that he wasn't. He must try another chair, and another, and another, until all were tried. By then, his whole body was one great ache, and his head was roaring, and his kidneys seemed to have been torn loose from his body. The worst pain, the worst indignity, was to his loins, where he had come down straddling a chair arm. Somehow, he managed to gasp out a request, and Pellino nodded and led him to a sink; stood there watching while he relieved himself. Then the torture was resumed.

He made the circuit of the room twice before Pellino was satisfied. Perhaps he would have made it again, but more was obviously unnecessary. More would have accomplished no more.

There was nothing left in him, nothing of what one needed to live. He had had very little to begin with, and now even that little was gone.

Studying him narrowly, drawing a chair up in front of him, Pellino wondered if he might have gone too far.

"Okay, Georgie?" he said, a trifle anxiously. "Think you got all the crap knocked out of your skull?"

"Eh? Oh, right-o. Quite," Carrington said.

"Then I'll cut you in on this McBride thing. Give you a piece off the top . . ."

"No need, old man. Can't say that it really interests me."

"Well"—Pellino took another look at him—"thought

you'd be better out of it, myself, but as long as the subject's come up. . . . Now, the lid's probably going to blow off on McBride; don't know why it hasn't already. But we've got to clamp it back on fast—we, not you; you don't know nothing. We've got to have a cinch, and we're lining one up. A way of tossing it under the carpet and stomping it down, without a peep or a wiggle. No investigations. No battling back and forth, with a lot of side issues being dragged in. You get me, George? You see why it has to be that way, why we can't have some private eye or screwball like you messing into it?"

"Oh, quite," said Carrington vacantly. "Right-o, check, and all that rot."

"Good," said Pellino, but he didn't sound certain that it was. "Like a drink, Georgie? Like to lie down a while?"

Carrington declined with courteous flatness. "Just brush up a bit, if you don't mind. Lave the old jowls."

"You do that," Pellino said. "Me, I think I'll take that drink."

Carrington bathed his face at the sink; combed his mussed, graying brown hair. He straightened out his tie and carefully adjusted his rumpled clothes. Pellino watched him, his small eyes worried and wondering.

Smiling warmly, outwardly himself again, Carrington faced around from the sink.

"Well, must toddle on, I suppose. Thanks for everything, old man."

"Thank . . . Oh, yeah, sure, Georgie," Pellino said; then, "Look, George, tell me something, will you?"

"But, of course. Anything I can."

"Well, look. What—how did you see the picture when we first showed it to you? You know, back when you opened the door for us and we moved in on you. Didn't you smell anything, Georgie? Did you figure we were tossing all that bread in your lap just because you were hungry?"

Carrington hesitated, puzzling out the translation of bread and hungry. He laughed his polite little laugh. "Think I may have, old man. Quite understandable, you know."

"*Understandable,* Georgie?"

"Understandable to me. Sort of thing I'd 've done myself if our positions had been reversed. Say I had scads of the old gilt, and I see some nice chap struggling against terrific odds and sinking in the sea of life, et cetera et cetera. Must give him a hand-up, what? Can't just sit on the jolly life preserver when it's so simple to toss it to him."

He smiled brightly, palm extended in a so-there-you-are gesture. Pellino came slowly to his feet, his body trembling with sudden unreasoning fury.

"You dumb son of a bitch," he snarled. "You scram out of here, get me? Beat it, and don't you ever come back! You show your stupid pan out here again, and——"

"Oh, I won't," Carrington promised. "Scout's oath, honor bright, and all that rot."

*　　*　　*

Taxiing back into the city, Carrington looked out into the gathering night and was completely relaxed and content for the first time in a long, long time. It had been a truly wonderful day, he thought. A truly jolly day. Mrs. McBride had proved to be a terrifically nice person—amazingly understanding and considerate. And how could anyone have been more pleasant than Mr. Pellino? Yet he had actually rather dreaded seeing both!

It just went to show how wrong a chap could be about people. Not too pure in heart himself, p'raps—that must be it, mustn't it?—so he suspected them. Whereas, on the other hand, if one's own auricles and ventricles were properly scrubbed, then he had nothing to fear and so on or something.

"My soul it has the strength of ten," he murmured, "because my—my, uh—hands are clean." Or was that right? Never could remember those jolly old rhymes. Maybe it was, uh—

AND JUDAS WEPT, SAYING, YEAH, VERILY I ABOMINATE ONIONS YET I CAN NEVER WITHSTAND THEM.

Silly. That wasn't it, of course. How did those silly things pop into a chap's mind?

The cab drew up at the entrance of a downtown office building. Carrington got out, pressed a five-dollar bill into the driver's hand, and curled his fingers around it.

"You're a wonderful man," he said warmly, "I can see it in your eyes. A truly beautiful and wonderful man."

"Yeah?" The driver jerked his hand away. "Well, you better line yourself up something else, buddy. I'm workin' tonight."

"Oh, right," said Carrington. "Going to be rather busy myself."

The cigar-stand clerk, a new man on the job, was locking up for the night. Carrington took a package of mints from the carton on the counter, and refused the change from a ten-dollar bill. "You deserve it," he said. "You deserve the best of everything."

The clerk examined the bill suspiciously, saw that it was good, and quickly palmed it. "Look, mister," he said, "take it kind of easy, huh? I don't know how you got away from your keeper, but——"

"Oh, I didn't get away from him," Carrington said. "Have him with me all the time."

He rode up to the nineteenth floor, one-half of which was now occupied by Highlands. As he stepped off the elevator, he gave the operator a twenty-dollar bill, the last of his money. The boy accepted it reluctantly, along with Carrington's assurances of his goodness.

"Let me get you some coffee out of it, anyway, Mr. Carrington. A big carton of black coffee, and maybe a sandwich. That'll snap you out of it."

Carrington declined with thanks. "Not at all hungry, laddie. Hardly decent to gorge at such a time, anyway."

The biggest and best of Highlands' offices were devoted

to the legal and accounting departments. Carrington's was in the rear, facing the alley; a cubbyhole similar to the one he had occupied in his pre-Pellino days.

Carrington entered it, flung open the French windows, and stepped through them.

10

Tom Lord drove away from Joyce Lakewood's cottage with that rare good feeling a man has when he has been persuaded to do exactly what he wanted. Sobering up the last couple days, getting off the booze entirely, he had decided to get away from Big Sands for a while. Not far away, not splendidly away, but just away. There was nothing to hold him here now—although, of course, he must come back. He could not picture himself as living permanently in another place. But for the time being, he needed a change. And it was the one need, among his many, which he was able to satisfy.

He had been about to tell Joyce of his decision, to suggest that she might like to accompany him, when she herself had begun to hint at just such an excursion. And Lord, knowing her nature, had immediately put on a long face and demurred.

"But you should get away, Tom! It would be good for you."

"Maybe. Hard to say. Be a lot of trouble for you, though."

"No, it wouldn't, honey! Honestly! I'd love to do it."

"Well, that's different," Lord drawled. "You want to do it, why, I will. Just for you, baby."

Joyce kissed him delightedly. He did lov—like her a lot, didn't he? More than anyone else?

"Hell, don't it look like it?" Lord said. "Catch me pulling up stakes on a minute's notice for any other gal."

He left her glowing with happiness, babbling with a thousand plans for their trip. He was to hurry right back, now. Just as soon as he could pack a bag. And she'd be ready when he got back.

Lord promised, feeling pretty good himself, only faintly disturbed by the fact that having seemingly won her way in this matter, she was hopeful of a still greater victory. Because she obviously was hopeful. She was keeping it corked up, trying not to show it, but he could see it just the same. Which meant that she was building herself up for a hell of a letdown. But that was her fault, not his.

He wasn't marrying her. He wasn't marrying anyone, and he particularly wasn't marrying her.

A man—a Lord, anyway—couldn't. He couldn't go through life wondering how many of the guys he passed had laid his wife. He didn't hold her past against her; everyone had a reason for being what he was, and she doubtless had hers. But he couldn't live with that past. She shouldn't expect him to become a partner in it.

The Lord residence was in the old-family section of Big

Sands, a single long row of houses overlooking the town from a gentle slope. The newest of the twenty-odd homes there was more than sixty years old, and most had been built in the Civil War era or earlier, yet all were of such reserved architecture—the commodious, clean-lined American Plains school—and all had been so well-constructed with no sparing of time and expense that none seemed dated, none was even incipiently run-down or wearing out.

The Lord home, one of three houses in its block, occupied a corner, with grounds stretching some seventy-five yards along the street. Despite the perpetual scarcity of water the lawn was always green, when the seasons permitted; the shrubs and trees were always nourished and flourishing. Imbedded in the roadside hitching block and affixed to the front door of the house were bronze plates with the identical legend:

Thomas DeMontez Lord, M.D.
Physician and Surgeon

Lord's great-grandfather had put the plates in place. His son and his grandson, both bearing the name, both following the same profession, had left them there. And the last of his line, ex-Deputy Sheriff Thomas DeMontez Lord, had never thought of removing them. They belonged there. They were not his to remove.

With the coming of the boom, the plates brought an occasional intruder, newcomers looking for a doctor and encouraged to walk in by the hospitably unlocked front door. But Lord regarded this as rather amusing, and no real bother at all. And he saw no reason to change his ways or break with tradition because of it.

The plates remained where they had been put. The doors remained unlocked. And strangers continued to stray inside. As he entered the house today, paused in the doorway of his father's office, he saw that still another had come in. She was a pretty little gal, he thought. Cute as a bug's ear and just about as tiny, but with proper amounts of meat in all the right places. Awful peaked-looking, though. Seemed to have just enough blood in her to pink up her mouth and put a spot on each cheek.

"Excuse me, ma'am," he said, looking her over impassively. "Were you waitin' to see the doctor?"

"Well, no. No, I wasn't." She half-came to her feet. "I wanted to see his son—that is, I guess it would be his son. Tom Lord . . . ?"

The statement came out as a question. She found herself smiling weakly, already pleading and placatory when there was no reason at all to be. She had a right to be here. She certainly had the right to come to this town, to press the investigation into Aaron's murder. But while these people— all of them out here—did not deny that right, neither did they concede it. They volunteered nothing. They looked at you and through you, as though you had no real substance. And if you blew up and lost your temper, as she had already done once today, they remained completely unmoved. Coolly polite, laconically impassive. Silently demanding that you justify yourself, while they decided what should be done about you.

"Tom Lord," she said firmly. "I want to see Tom Lord."

"Yes, ma'am?"

"Yes! Can you tell me where I can find him?"

"Might be I could. What'd you want to see him about, ma'am?"

"About m-my, my——" Her head swam with sudden dizziness, and she sank back on the lounge. "P-lease," she said. "Can't you answer a simple question? Can't anyone in this crazy place answer a question without asking one?"

"Yes, ma'am. Can you?"

"Can——? All right," she sighed. "I'm Mrs. Donna McBride. My husband, Aaron McBride, was recently killed out in the fields. I want to talk to Mr. Lord about his death."

"Tom's not a deputy any more, ma'am. Seems like you ought to talk to the sheriff."

"I know he's not a deputy, and I did talk to the sheriff! I talked to him and all those other stupid oafs that're supposed to be officers, deputies, and they were as bad as you are! Worse even! I almost exhausted myself just finding out where Mr. Lord lived!"

"Maybe they figured Mr. Lord didn't want to see you."

"But I—I——!" She wanted to yell. In fact, she realized, she had been yelling. "Please," she said, fighting down the swelling hysteria, struggling up from the growing dizziness. "Please. I can't tell you exactly why I want to see Mr. Lord. I'm not completely sure myself, and I just don't know why I should. It's between Mr. Lord and me."

"You mean it's none of my business, ma'am?"

"Well . . . frankly, no, it isn't."

"Reckon I better not butt into it then, had I? Shouldn't be asking me to."

She stared at him, dully, despairingly. He looked back at her, his expression blankly polite. Or—or was it completely so? Wasn't there a trace of amusement, of mockery, in the cool dark eyes.

"All right," she said, her voice shaky with weakness. "I'll go now. You won't help me. No one in this rotten, filthy place will help me. Just where anyone ever got the notion that Westerners were p-polite and courteous is—is——"

She faltered, the blackness rolling over her in a wave.

"Yes, ma'am?" he said. "Maybe they got it from people that was polite and courteous themselves."

Another black wave hit her. When she floated up out of it, she was lying on the lounge, and he was seated on its edge looking down at her.

"You shouldn't be up wandering around, ma'am. Not so soon after a Caesarean."

"Oh . . ." She blushed, tugged primly at her skirt. "Then, you're Doctor Lord?"

"Might say I was a reasonable facsimile, thereof, ma'am. Now, you just stay here a minute. Goin' to give you a little shot of something."

He prepared a hypodermic. These many years after Dr. Lord's death, he still received samples from the various medical supply houses.

He rolled up her sleeve, sponged her arm. As he started to inject the hypo, she tried to pull away from him.

"This won't put me to sleep, will it, Doctor?"

"Well"—he depressed the hypo plunger, completed the injection—"Well, yes, ma'am. Give you the good sound rest you need."

"But I can't! I mustn't! I've got to see Tom Lord!"

"Oh, you'll see him, ma'am. And he'll see you." He grinned at her impishly, his voice following her down into the void in which she was swiftly descending. "Yes, sir, he'll see a lot of you . . . literally and figuratively."

Her brows knitted in drowsy puzzlement. Her eyes drifted open for a moment, stared into his. She blushed faintly, and a tiny, half-shamed giggle arose in her throat.

Then she was asleep.

Lord carried her upstairs, and into a bedroom. He carried her to the bed, and paused in the act of laying her down.

She needed rest, this little lady. Not just for a few hours, but at least several days. And the way she was bundled up, she sure couldn't do much of a job resting. Felt like she had so damned many duds on—slips and underskirts and God-knew-what-all—that they weighed more than she did. And he wondered whether all these cumbersome trappings of modesty were her own idea or McBride's.

Well, no matter. She had to come out of them, and there was no one but him to get her out.

He did so with awkward efficiency, laying her across his lap in baby-burping fashion and peeling the garments off over her head and down over her feet. Then, digging down into an ancient cedar chest, he came up with a tissue-paper-wrapped armful of gossamer silk and lace.

Its faint fragrance drifted up to him, and for a moment he was back in that long-ago night, in the dream that had been a reality. And a haunted, hungry look came into his eyes. He stood almost motionless, hugging the silk and lace against him, fighting to bring back, to hold onto something that was gone forever. Finally, seeing himself in the tall, mahogany-framed mirror, he was jerked back into the present.

He laughed harshly. He made his selections from the garments, tossed the others back into the cedar chest, and kicked the lid down on them.

Dressing Donna McBride in his mother's nightgown and negligee, he was struck by how well they fitted. As though they had been made for her almost. As though they—she was—and he angrily slammed the door on the thought. So they were the same size. What the hell of it? A lot of women had the same full but delicate build, and it didn't mean a damned thing. It had nothing to do with his feelings about Donna McBride, or why he was treating her as he was.

She was ill. Having killed her husband, he was responsible for her; he had to take care of her. And he also had to find out just how much she knew about Tom Lord, and exactly what she intended to do about it.

The last wasn't too hard to guess; that is, if she knew nothing but the bald truth without the circumstances that went with it. Maybe the circumstances wouldn't make any difference to a little hardhead like her anyway. Doubtless they wouldn't. Her presence here indicated her attitude, her belief that McBride had been killed. And judging by the weight of her purse, she was all set to take care of his killer.

He opened the purse, and verified his assumption. He hefted the small, fully loaded pistol. It was brand, spanking new; bought, apparently, for just one purpose.

So . . . ?

So he had to stick with her, keep an eye on her. Try to divert her or reason with her, or set up some defense for himself. He had to do it. Otherwise, he damned well wouldn't be doing it. For in trying to stave off the danger which she represented, he was laying himself wide open to as great a peril in Joyce Lakewood.

He was already overdue back at Joyce's house. Joyce would be all saddled up and champing at the bit by now. Any minute she'd be phoning to ask why the hell the hold up, telling him to get going like he'd promised. And when he told her that the trip was off, indefinitely, if not per-manently—this trip which meant so much to her and which she was already regarding as a prelude to marriage . . .

She wouldn't take it. She wouldn't take any excuses. She'd cry and she'd beg, and then she'd get sore. Blind, crazy mad. And pretty soon after that she'd be talking to Sheriff Dave Bradley. Putting him in a spot where he'd have to do something about the killing and the killer of Aaron McBride.

She'd be sorry about it afterward. But the damage would be done then.

The phone rang.

He hurried out of the room, pulled the door shut, and picked up the hall extension.

"Hello," he said. "Oh, hi, Joyce."

"Tom! For Pete's sake, honey, what's holding you up? I've been waiting and waiting, and——"

"Look, Joyce. Listen," he cut in guardedly. "I can't talk right now. I mean, I don't want to do a lot of talkin' over the telephone. But——"

"I don't want to do a lot of talking either!" She was already sore; intuitively, she saw that her plans were fading away. "I want you to get over here right now, and you'd better come!"

"And I'm trying to tell you I can't. We can't make that trip, Joyce. Not for a while, anyways. I'll try t' get over an' explain in a few days, but——"

"Wh-aat? What do you mean we can't. . . . You'd better explain right now, damn you! I'm not going to believe it anyway, but you get over here or I'm coming over there!"

"Huh-uh," he said, his temper flickering. "I'm not, and you're not. You ain't coming anywhere near here. I told you I was sorry, an' you oughta know I——"

She broke in with an angry sob; she bawled. Lord fidgeted fretfully.

"Now, looky, Joyce. We talked about all we better, so——"

"Don't you hang up on me, Tom Lord! You just try it and see what happens."

"Swell," said Lord, "and maybe after I see what happens, you'll see what happens."

He hung up. Almost immediately, the phone rang again.

"Now, you listen to me, Tom. I'm going to wait just thirty minutes for you to get over here. No, I'll wait an hour. If . . ."

"You do that," Lord said. "Try holdin' your breath while you're waiting."

He slammed down the receiver.

The phone did not ring again.

Fat August Pellino was hard-hit by the suicide of George Carrington. The news was hardly in the papers before he received a series of guarded long-distance calls, followed by an equal number of visitors to his old-fashioned brick residence.

Always before, when there was need for a conference, Augie had called it. Otherwise, his business associates had left him strictly alone. This time, however, they had simply announced they were coming, advising him to hold himself in readiness. And in their action, Pellino saw the faint outlines of the handwriting on the wall.

He was no longer in the saddle—at least, he was not seated in it firmly. He was teetering, and the slightest jostle, the smallest move of the wrong kind, would find him dumped in the dust.

Mrs. Pellino prepared an elaborate old-country feast for the group. There was much bowing and scraping and exchanging of compliments; much embracing and fluid laughter. Pellino took part in it, but uncomfortably, with barely concealed impatience. He had never gone for this stuff. He had never liked these people, whom he thought of as wops. He was Sicilian himself, on his father's side, but he was essentially his mother's son. Essentially, he was Prussian rather than Latin.

At last, the formal feasting and gabbing was over. Mrs. Pellino vanished into the upper reaches of the house, and Augie and his guests retired to the basement. Bottles were opened, cigars passed. Augie found himself seated alone on one of the long leather lounges, and somehow a light had been focused on him. His associates, on the other hand, sat half in the shadows, ringing him in a seemingly casual semi-circle.

There was silence. It grew deeper and deeper. Pellino wanted to rip out a curse, to get up and start swinging at those blandly impassive faces. And he knew it would be the end of him if he did. For this silence—the treatment—was intended to provoke just some such outburst; to bring out any signs of weakness—or guilt—that might be in a man. And if such were revealed, the man was not allowed to slip from the saddle. He was knocked from it.

Pellino wondered who his successor would be, and he saw, or rather sensed, that the man had already been elected. He was from New Jersey, and his name was Salvatore Onate; one of the oldest of the group and undoubtedly the most prosperous. Obviously, there had been some kind of meeting prior to this one, and Sal had been named spokesman and leader in waiting.

The silence went on and on. August waited, as calmly

quiet outwardly as his guests. There was a sudden, tinkling crash, and he jumped. Involuntarily, he half-rose from the lounge.

A ripple of soft laughter ran through the room. Salvatore Onate smiled apologetically.

"How clumsy of me, August. I'm afraid I broke one of your glasses."

Pellino was furious, but he managed a half-polite gesture of dismissal. The glass was a cheap thing, really, and Sal should leave it where it had fallen.

"Perhaps that would be best," Onate nodded gravely. "After all, who can put together a broken glass?"

"Who indeed?" said Pellino.

He was prepared to outwait and outtalk this old bastard as long as it was necessary. *Dropping that glass, damn him; deliberately taking him for a rise!* But the younger men had little patience for this kind of game, and Onate noted their growing restlessness.

"Now, we should get down to business, Gus," he said, his voice growing curt. "We got a lot of dough parked with you. It don't look to us like you're taking very good care of it."

"So how ain't I?" Pellino shrugged. "Maybe you ain't looking at it right."

"He's looking at it right!" snapped Carlos Moroni, the Chicago man. "Two so-called suicides in less than a month! Two big-shots from the same company, and not a very big company at that! This is smart? You think you can crap all over the landscape without raising a stink?"

Pellino glowered at him. He snarled that he had neither directly nor indirectly caused the deaths of Carrington and McBride, and the police were quite content to accept them as suicides.

"How the hell you know they are?" sneered the Los Angeles representative. "Did they write you a letter? How you know the roof ain't about to fall in on us right now?"

"Because there's no goddamned reason for it to!"

"Conceding," said Sal Onate, "that the suicides were legitimate . . . and we are not at all sure that you are without guilt in the Carrington matter . . ."

"What"—Pellino swallowed—"what do you mean by that?"

"Don't play dumb," said Moroni. "What the hell would we mean? You ask me, we ought to've been keeping tabs on you a lot sooner."

There were nods of agreement to this. A strangling tightness came into Pellino's throat. The situation was far worse than he had thought. Apparently, he had been under surveillance for months.

"All right," he said, "Carrington was out here to the house. Just a little while before he died. But no one knew about it."

"We knew about it."

"But I didn't have nothing to do with his getting killed! He was by himself when it happened. Sure, I was sore about his coming out here. Sure, I tossed him around a little. So what?"

"Let it go," said Onate, with seeming idleness. "You had

nothing to do with it. You are not probably responsible for McBride's death. Now, what about this officer, the man Thomas Lord?"

"What about him? He got rooked and he's sore. So what?"

"Then everything is fine, yes?" Onate nodded, his tone still idle. "Our investment is safe. There is nothing to fear."

"Well . . . sure. You can add it up for yourself."

"But we have had no return on the investment, Gus. Practically none. It has all been plowed back into the business, along with our original capital."

"So you know the answer to that. Look at the new drilling rigs we bought, and them things cost! Better than two hundred grand a rig! We bought tanks and trucks and——"

"How much would they bring at a forced sale? Assuming, that is, that such a sale was possible."

"How much?" Pellino frowned. "I don't get you, Sal."

But, of course, he did get it, and they knew that he did. The possibility of investigation had at last made them see the danger which he had seen in the beginning. Highlands had been racing against time. The oil had had to be gotten out of the ground very quickly. Thus, the huge and constant investment in new equipment—equipment which, as salvage, would not bring a fraction of its original cost.

"Our holdings," said Sal Onate, "have a book value of more than five million dollars. We suggest that you sell them."

"Sell them! But——"

"But you can't," Onate nodded. "The title to our principal leases—and, of course, everything attached to them and deriving from them—is clouded. No one but a fool would buy them at even the most modest price."

Pellino hesitated, trying to protest. Then, feebly, he spread his hands. "All right, Sal; you called the turn. But things have been that way right from the beginning."

"No. They are not as they were in the beginning. Neither McBride nor Carrington was dead then—both under suspicious circumstances. Nor is Lord the man which you represented him as being. He is not a bumbling, small-town clown, but an intelligent and determined man; a trouble maker of the worst kind. At one time, perhaps, he could have been bought off reasonably. But now . . ."

He shook his head, leaving the sentence unfinished. Pellino said hopefully that it was still worth a try. But he was far from sure that it was, and uncertainty was in his voice.

As yet, apparently, Lord hadn't fully appreciated the strength of his position. But any gesture of appeasement was apt to open his eyes, and his reaction was more than apt to be disastrous.

"So all right," said Pellino, "maybe we don't make him no offer. Maybe it wouldn't be smart."

"And?"

"What do you think? He's a loner, no heirs or kin. He ain't around any more, we got no worries."

It was easily his worst blunder. Onate gave him a look of frowning incredulity. Carlos Moroni snorted, jerking a contemptuous thumb at him.

"Get this Pellino, will you? Like some half-assed mystery writer! He don't know what the hell to do, so he has everyone drowned in a flood."

"Very stupid, Gus," sighed Sal Onate. "Two deaths, two that could have been murder, and now you suggest a third. Killing a man who is not only identified with Highlands, but also associated with the law. If this is an example of your thinking . . ."

"The stupid son of a bitch don't think at all!" snapped the Los Angeles man. And then they were all talking at once.

He had done nothing right. Every move he had made, seemingly shrewd at the time, was now cited as a blunder. Mrs. McBride was suspicious. Lord had declared a vendetta. Highlands had a dangerously ugly reputation in the fields. Danger loomed from every side; the danger of exposure and the danger of losing their entire investment. And for the great risks they had taken and were taking, they had received no payment whatsoever. When there had been a sizable pot to split, Pellino had dumped it into an exploratory well. Seventy thousand dollars sunk into the ground, with a string of tools irretrievably jammed on top of it.

"And according to our geological reports," said Sal Onate severely, "there was no oil there in the first place. It was simply more of our money thrown away."

Pellino's temper flickered, then wearily subsided. It was their right to check on him. And checking, they would naturally check on that wildcat well; on anything that might be misfeasance or malfeasance, betrayal or blunder. They were always thorough, men like these. They did not act without ample evidence.

"Well, Gus?" said Onate. "Well?"

Pellino stalled, carefully relighting his cigar and carefully blowing out the match.

"Well, how about it?" said Moroni. "You got something to say or not?"

August looked at him coolly, took a long puff from his cigar, and spewed a stream of smoke at him. "I've got something to say. You want to listen, or do you want to jump down my throat?"

"Talk!"

Pellino talked. He declared that he had never had any intention of hitting Lord; in suggesting that Lord be got out of the way, he had meant only that. Either to have him lured and kept away peaceably, or to have him framed. With the contact he had in Big Sands one or the other should be a cinch.

"Contact!" Moroni spat. "Now, there's a fancy name for a whore. Five million bucks, and he's bettin' it on a double-crossing whore!"

"Now, Carlos," said Onate mildly. "Whores can be very useful. . . . You can manage this quickly, Gus?"

"Why not?"

"Good. It is settled, then."

The meeting broke up shortly after that. When his guests had departed, Pellino repaired to the kitchen, sat there drinking coffee and staring sourly into nothingness. He was by no means sure that he could get rid of Lord. He had simply been talking off the top of his head, making promises because he had to. Given enough time, he could doubtless dispose of Lord in a way that would be free of kickbacks. But he had virtually no time; he had to rush in without any time for laying a proper groundwork. And such tactics seldom resulted in success.

He brooded. His mind moved over the events of the evening, the insults and the threats, and his fat face purpled with rage. His associates had known the risk they were taking right from the beginning. He had made very sure that they understood it. The lease titles were clouded; they could only be realized upon by being rapidly drilled-up and selling off the oil. All of this had been known by all; yet, now, when the always potential peril seemed about to become actual—and through no fault of his. . . .

It was a bad shake. He had been damned, and tentatively doomed, even before the meeting tonight. Without his knowledge, a new president of Highlands had been appointed, a man from the accounting department. Also without his knowledge, a new field boss had been hired. Briefly, he, Gus Pellino, no longer had a voice in Highlands' affairs. He had the full responsibility for the company's welfare—oh, sure, he had that, all right!—but no authority.

Just wait. Pellino raged silently. *Just wait until I'm back on top again, and they come sucking around me!*

They knew no tricks that he didn't know. He knew how to dig up dirt which, exhibited to a man's enemies, could easily prove fatal to him. And just as soon as he was in the clear. . . !

Slowly, his eyes raised toward the ceiling, and his thoughts moved upward with them—up there to the bedroom, where his wife lay in the moonlit darkness, she of the blankly pleasant smile and the rich and willing body. Their marriage had been one largely of convenience, a means of strengthening ties which were always a little tenuous. (*And a hell of a lot of good it did when the chips were down!*) It had seemed, at the time, that he was mainly the gainer by the deal. But now he was no longer so sure.

Yes or no? he thought. *Had she or hadn't she?*

He shrugged, arose from the table, and went heavily up the stairs. He had nothing to lose by seeking out the truth. If he took care of Lord satisfactorily, nothing else would matter. If he failed, nothing else would matter. In the larger scheme of things, she was merely another old-country relative, of which there was already a burdensome abundance.

As he entered the room, she awakened and smiled at him, moved slightly over in the bed. He sat down at her side, started to pull down her nightgown, and she hastened to help him. Her breasts seemed to leap into his hands. He began to stroke them, gently at first, then with ominously increasing firmness.

"You have a nice time, *cara*? It was good to see your kinsmen?"

"*Sì?*" She didn't understand him. Apparently, she didn't. "You say wot, Gossie?"

Pellino grinned at her. His fingers dug in suddenly, her lightly blue-veined flesh squeezing up between them, and she squirmed slowly on the narrow border between agony and ecstasy.

"P-please, Gossie. A leetle it is all right. I like even. But s-so moch—*Gossie!*"

"Can't understand nothin', hmmm?" Pellino grunted. "Can't talk to me, can you? Not to me. But Uncle Sal, now—him and Cousin Carlos—they're something else again, ain't they? You can talk plenty to them!"

"P-please," she gasped, writhing. "G-Gossie . . . w'y you do thees?"

Pellino's hands twisted cruelly. He told her she had better figure it out, and do it fast.

"I mean it, sister! You go on playin' dumb, and I'll pull them tits right off of you."

"B-but I do not—I cannot——"

"Okay," Pellino gritted. "Maybe you can grow a new pair."

She moaned, half-screamed. She surged upward from the bed, and then fell back upon the bed. Her eyelids fluttered and drifted shut. Her lips moved inaudibly.

"Snap out of it"—he bent over her. "Let's hear——"

Then, he jerked away from her, wiping the spittle from his face.

Her perpetually pleasant smile was gone now, replaced by the hard lines of hatred. Gone, too, was the puzzled blankness of her eyes, where hatred now glittered.

She put her right thumb in her mouth, up to the first

joint. She withdrew it suddenly, flicking it at him. She said nothing. She did not need to.

Without speaking, she had told him the truth.

"I'm going out of town, now," he said. "Leaving as soon as I pack a bag. You want to pass the word to your kin, it's all right with me."

"I will tell them to kill you!"

"They won't do it. Not for you, anyhow." He nodded indifferently; a man stating the axiomatic with a casualness that was utterly convincing. "They needed you. Now, they don't. And I figure they got about as much use for a two-timer as I have."

He let the words sink in: the fact that she was inextricably bound to him, and that after him there would be no one. It was incredible, terrifying—how could her own kinsmen have done this to her?—but there it was. Treachery would be repaid with treachery.

"Gossie," she tried to smile. "I did not mean it, Gos. They misled me, made me think I was helping you."

"We'll see," Pellino told her. "We'll talk about it when I get back. Maybe we'll have us a nice little party, huh? You know—party? Just the two of us."

"Oh, yes, Gossie!" She clutched eagerly for his hand, and found it withdrawn. "A ver' nice party."

"Good," said Pellino. "You can kind of be preparing for it while I'm away. Lay in a supply of linament, bandages, and stuff. You're going to need them."

Then he got up, went through the door, and closed it quietly behind him.

12

For the tenth time in almost as many minutes, Tom Lord paused in his nervous pacing of the floor and looked at his watch. It was afternoon, now, nearly midafternoon. It had been hours since Joyce's last call, when he had literally invited her to do her damndest. Yet nothing had happened. No visit from the sheriff. Nothing.

He wandered out into the kitchen, and peered vaguely out the window. He got a drink of water at the sink; then, hardly aware of what he was doing, he chased it with a shot of bourbon from the cupboard. Aimlessly, he crossed to the refrigerator and inspected its contents. The sight of the food brought a frown to his face, and he listened worriedly for some sound from the upstairs.

"No telling when she ate last," he muttered aloud. "No food and a hell of a big hypo. . . ."

She needed to snap out of it, he decided. She needed some grub in her.

Or maybe, he chuckled grimly, *I need to be doing something. Maybe I've really been begging for trouble all along, and I just can't wait for it to hit me.*

He laughed at the thought. The laugh ended abruptly; an incipient monster strangled in its fetal stage. Quickly, he threw down another big drink of the bourbon, shuddering at its sudden, flaming impact. Then he busied himself with the food. He put bread into the toaster. He put milk, eggs, whisky and sugar into a bowl, and flicked on the electric mixer. Some ten minutes later, he pushed open the bedroom door, set the tray down on a chair, and brought Donna McBride into wakefulness.

It wasn't difficult. The drug had worn off, and her sleep was natural. He propped pillows behind her back, winked encouragingly, and put the tray on her lap.

He ordered her to eat. Obediently, responding to the authority in his voice, she began to.

The toast disappeared rapidly. She couldn't remember when anything had tasted so good to her. She took a sip of the milkish-looking drink, frowned slightly at its taste, then, shrugging inwardly, took a large swallow. It *was* good. It tasted good, and it made her feel good—all warm and nice, and sort of ticklish. And if it did have a little alcohol in it—and she was by no means sure that it did—well, it was only medicine if a doctor gave it to you.

She drank the last of the glass, a delicate flush spreading over her face. At any minute, she felt, she was going to burst out giggling. Yet, as the urge grew, her habitual reserve, the inbred primness, reasserted itself.

"Doctor," she said severely, "you put whisky in that drink, didn't you? Quite a lot of it."

"*Whisky!*" Lord registered pained astonishment. "Whisky? Oh, that I should live to see this moment!"

"Now, you stop that!" she said. "Stop it right now. I appreciate your help, Doctor, but I'm afraid I don't care for your professional behavior. Why, I shouldn't even be here like—like this—without your nurse present."

"Nurse?" Lord elevated his brows. "But I ain't got no nurse, ma'am. Wouldn't hardly be no point to it, seein' as how I ain't a doctor."

"Not a——!" She broke off, very conscious suddenly of the sheer nightgown, burningly aware that it must have been he who had transposed her into it from her own clothes. "B-but you said——" But he hadn't said it; only something about being a reasonable facsimile of a doctor. "Who are you?" she demanded.

"Fella you was lookin' for. Tom Lord."

"Tom L-Lord!" She stared at him angrily. "Why didn't you tell me so in the beginning?"

"Reckon you might be able to think of a reason yourself. What are you kickin' about, anyway? Ain't many gals I'd put to bed in my mama's own nightshirt."

Donna spluttered. On the point of exploding with fury, she caught herself, and studied him curiously. What was the matter with him, anyhow? Why was he acting like this? He could have appeased her, lied to her, carried on the masquerade of being a doctor. Instead, he seemed determined to aggravate and insult her.

"Mr. Lord," she said. "Are you . . . are you all right?"

"You mean am I crazy?" Lord studied the question soberly. "I don't know," he said, after a moment. "Could be, I guess. Or it could be I just don't like to wait for things to happen to me."

"Wait? What——"

"Uh-huh. I don't like to wait, but I ain't got the guts to bring things to an outright showdown. Kind of a two-way pull, you know, or maybe, three-way or four-way. I don't like nothin' like it is, and I don't really want to change it. So I just keep circlin' the target, wherever the hell it is. I just gnaw around the edges without ever gettin' close to center."

Donna looked at him, her own problems and her anger with him forgotten for the moment. Then, as she felt a sudden compelling weakness flood over her, she gave her head an irritable little shake. This wouldn't do at all. She had come here for information, not to lie in bed and listen to a lot of foolishness.

"Mr. Lord," she said crisply. "I'd like to dress. Do you hear me, Mr. Lord?"

He lost his dreamy, thoughtful look; the oddly dancing lights came back into his eyes. He said that sure, he heard her, and she was to go right ahead and dress. "O' course," he added, "you're liable to doze off a-fore you get your panties on."

"Mr. Lord!" she snapped. "I said I wanted to dress. I want you to leave the room!"

"What for?" Lord drawled. "Ain't gonna see nothin' I ain't already seen. Not unless you've growed something new since I put you to bed."

She looked at him helplessly, sank weakly back into the pillows. She wanted to cry, and oddly enough, to laugh, and she could only succumb to the drowsiness.

"A fine thing," she said. "You were supposed to be my husband's friend, and——"

"Me? *His* friend!" Lord exclaimed; and then, thoughtfully, "Well, maybe I was. Don't reckon there's anyone else that'd think so, but . . ."

"He thought you were, b-but look how you act. I came to you for help, and all you can do is joke and t-talk dirty, and——" Her voice broke.

Lord's face contorted, and suddenly he was down on his knees at her side. Hugging her to him fiercely. "Aah, no, honey," he whispered. "I didn't mean it that way. I just . . . I was always a little odd, remember? You remember, don't you? Even when I was a toddler, and you used to . . ."

He broke off, came out of her drowsily unconscious embrace with something that was close to desperation. He stood looking down at her, slowly getting control of himself.

He would have to talk to her, eventually. Sooner or later, he would have to face up to the gun she carried. But not now, thank God. Not now. For she had gone to sleep, at last. Gone, as the other one had gone, into a world beyond his reach. And not a moment too soon either.

A car had pulled into the driveway. A rattly old car with a familiar piston slap.

Sheriff Dave Bradley had arrived.

13

Bradley had brought a deputy with him; gangling, moose-jawed Buck Harris. Lord awaited them in his father's old office, boots propped up on the desk, hands clasped behind his head.

Bradley was scowling importantly. Buck grinned at Lord uneasily, wishing that he was anywhere but here. Why, ol' Tom wouldn't do what that crazy gal claimed he had! It just wasn't in ol' Tom to kill a man in cold blood.

"Sure been missin' you down to the office, Tom," he said, just as the sheriff started to speak. "Don't seem like the same place no more without you around."

"Don't it?" Lord gave him a flat-eyed look. "Is that a fact, now?"

Buck said that, no, sir, it sure didn't seem the same— again speaking before the sheriff could. "You remember that hawg thief I nailed out t' the commission pens. Well, now he's claimin' he ain't guilty."

"He prob'ly ain't," Lord said. "I figure you stole them hawgs yourself."

"Aw, now . . ." the big deputy grinned uncertainly. "That ain't very funny, Tom. Why for would I be stealin' hogs?"

"Prob'ly because you ain't got two dimes to rub together; ol' Dave here grabs everything for himself. An' you prob'ly wanted to get them big ugly teeth of yours fixed."

Buck was very sensitive about his teeth; he usually talked with a hand held to his mouth. The hand went there now, his face white with hurt, slow anger building in his eyes. And Tom Lord was hurt for him, winced with him. But this was the way it had to be played. He had cut loose, or rather been cut loose, from something. It was best for all concerned that the cut be clean.

"Don't pay the ornery cuss no mind, Buck," said Bradley angrily; and then, "Tom Lord, I'm arrestin' you for the murder of Aaron McBride."

"Yeah?" Lord drawled. "Who says I murdered him?"

Bradley told him, and the ex-chief deputy shook his head. "She's been threatenin' to do that. Got peeved with me, and this is her way of hittin' back. I figure she ain't much of a witness, Dave."

"What you figure don't count! Now, you want to come peaceable or you want it t'other way?"

"We-el . . ." Lord pursed his lips judiciously. "Why don't we make it the other way? Might be real interestin'."

Bradley blinked, his mouth gaping open. He looked uncertainly at Buck Harris, and the deputy drew his forty-five. "Might be interestin' at that," he said. "You better get movin', Tom."

"Huh-uh," said Lord. "What you fellas better do is call Miss Lakewood again. I figure she'll probably change her story."

"Yeah?"

"Yeah. Unless you want to chomp up that pistol with them big teeth o' yours. Because I'll sure as hell make you eat it."

It was too much for Buck Harris, well aware as he was of Tom's handiness at "scufflin'." It was more than he could or would take, even with the sheriff ordering him to lay off.

He came around the desk, the gun drawn back for a whipping blow to the skull. The gun came down in a vicious arc, and one of Lord's booted feet moved lazily into its path, and Buck's wrist smashed into it. He grunted, almost yelled with the pain. His arm went numb all the way to the shoulder, and the gun flew from his nerveless fingers. Lord caught it with another lazy motion, ejected the shells from it, and flung it back at him.

"Have another try," he invited. "Three tries an' you get to eat it."

There was some method behind this madness, he decided; a subconscious reasoning behind it. Joyce would need time to cool off—if, that is, she would cool off, and by stalling he was giving her time. And Bradley had made it easy for him. Old Dave was stubborn. Told to check on Joyce, he was practically a cinch not to do it.

"Well, Dave . . . Buck?" Lord looked jovially from one to the other. "Ain't callin' off our little game already, are we?"

Bradley mumbled a feebly stern command: Tom had better do as he was told and be quick about it. Buck painfully scooped up his gun from the floor, fumbled cartridges from his belt, and began to refill the chamber.

"We ain't callin' it off," he announced. "Just gonna change the rules a little."

Lord roared with laughter. It drowned out Bradley's alarmed orders for Buck to stop—for Tom to stop egging him on. Buck dropped into a crouch, took awkward aim with his left hand. Lord doubled with laughter, slapping his knees, and then suddenly, still bent forward, he sprang.

He rocketed out of the chair, his hard shoulders hurtling into Harris at the level of his boot tops. Buck's legs flew from under him, the gun again flew from his hand, and his big body crashed against the floor.

Bradley helped him to his feet; snatched up the gun and held onto it.

"Now, I'm gonna call that gal," he panted angrily, swinging the gun from one man to the other, "an' there better not be no trouble while I'm doin' it. I'm the boss here. . . . Hello, Miss Lakewood? This is Dave Bradley. I'm over here t' Tom Lord's house, an'——"

He broke off, listening, an angry but obviously relieved scowl wrinkling his face. He said, "But dang it! Why did you——"

He paused again as a crackling, apologetically defiant stream of words torrented over the wire. Finally, when she apparently stopped for breath, he gave her a grimly firm reproof. "Don't know whether you were lyin' the first time or now, ma'am. But it's a plain bad thing, however it is. Got plenty of reason t'haul you in an' file charges . . . Well, all right, then. I'll let it go this time. But you sure better watch your step from now on."

He slammed up the receiver.

He jerked his head toward Buck Harris, and Harris wobbled after him toward the door, a spattering trickle of blood trailing behind him.

Bradley went on through the door. Buck paused on the threshold, and slowly turned around.

He looked like a tortured puppy. He looked like a rabid dog. He looked all the hideous things that only a sensitive man can who has seen his friendship flouted and his trust betrayed.

Lord could not meet the look. Savagely, his eyes averted, he filed another indictment in the endless litigation of *Lord vs Lord*. Tom Lord—in Tom Lord's opinion—was a goddamned liar. He behaved as he did, not out of any necessity or compulsion, but simply because he was a no-good bastard, and his incessant rationalizations to the contrary were so much crap. There was no excuse for what he'd done. He'd simply felt like kicking asses, and poor old Buck had been handy.

"Buck," he said, still looking away from that terrible face. "I'm sorry. You want to pistol-whip me all over the courthouse steps, I'm givin' you the privilege."

A drop of blood oozed over Buck's overhung upper lip,

and down onto his teeth. He brushed at it with a frayed shirtsleeve, silently staring at the result. And then, with an almost polite little nod, he turned and left.

Lord sighed, on a note of exhaustion. Absently, he lighted a cigar, stood outside of himself as he puffed it; curiously considering the man at the desk.

Looked about like anyone else out here. Talked like them. Acted like them. *Was* like them except for what went on inside of him. And yet that, the last, was the most important thing of all, the only important thing when you got right down to cases. It was him, not what showed up on the surface. It was what made him love or hate, die or give death. Yet no one was aware of it; no one could diagram its workings or predict their results. Certainly he, the man it inclined and impelled, could not. The machinery had become too complex; too many moments had been added to its sum.

It was easy to believe, of course, that the irking contradictions of his own life justified almost anything he did. He'd had it tough all the way down the line. Obviously— obviously, to his own way of thinking—he was a classic case of the square plug in the round hole, and he should be excused where others should not. And, hell. How stupid and blind did you have to be to think that way? Everyone was unique particularly, but no one generally. Every man's life was a different road, but all paralleled one another. Everyone was a son of a bitch, everyone an angel, everyone both. A man couldn't go very wrong, probably in treating everyone like a good guy. At worst, he probably wouldn't catch the dirty end of the stick more than fifty per cent of the time—which was about the best he could do now.

Tom Lord roused himself, and arose from the desk.

He had to get moving. He had to get the hell out of here; to stave off or, perhaps, hasten the tide of events which already threatened to engulf him. He had to go from here to there, from where he was to where he was not, inevitably taking with him, of course, the circumstances which necessitated the move.

Tom Lord and Tom Lord had to be on their way, and philosophizing must wait until another time. There were things to be done—ah, so many things—before they left. And there was no time for the merely crucial.

Donna McBride was sleeping peacefully, and obviously would be for hours to come. He took her pulse, listened to her heartbeat. Gently, he pulled back her eyelids, and gently released them. She was all right. Nothing wrong with her that a good rest wouldn't cure.

It was around midnight when he left the house. Some six blocks away, as he was nearing the old-town business district, he deliberately stalled the car beneath a street light.

He had chosen the spot carefully. There were no houses for more than a block and a half behind him, and the car back there would have no legitimate reason for stopping. So it came on, moving at the discreet fifteen miles per hour which local ordinances demanded. It passed him, necessarily very close because of the intersection, and Lord got a glimpse of the driver.

Without appearing to, he kept an eye on the vehicle; watched as it turned in at the curb in front of a drugstore. Then, after stalling a minute or two longer, and repairing the car's fictitious difficulty, he slammed down the hood and drove on.

He was hardly a block past the drugstore when the other car hastily backed away from the curb, its driver momentarily sticking his head out the window. It trailed him at what the man apparently thought was a safe distance. And the gears of Lord's memory meshed, and a bell rang.

So he hadn't been dreaming. There had been a man there at Joyce's house, the same one who was following him; and in the light of his present actions, his presence at Joyce's house had a sinister aspect.

Joyce didn't "work" any more, but she had plenty of money. And this man—a nonresident—was on familiar terms with her.

Joyce had wanted him, Lord, out of town. It had been extremely important to her. And he, Lord, was obviously important to this man.

Lord's heart quickened; the deadness fell away from him, and his eyes sparkled with interest. *Now, why?* he mused. *Now, where the hell have I seen that mug before——*

The word *mug* did the trick. The gears of memory whirred again, and a clanging bell announced a jackpot.

Back when the boom began to build, he'd made Bradley

see the danger of a gangster influx, and Bradley had consented to the setting up of an identification department. He wouldn't authorize any money for it, of course, since the taxpayers had none to waste on "frills." He was also very watchful of any time which any of his men might devote to it. About the only one willing to help was Buck Harris, a man who was patently as useless to such an enterprise as tits on a stud horse. So Lord had warded off his persistent offers of assistance, and done what had to be or could be done himself. The result naturally left something to be desired. One man couldn't swing the whole load, and the other police organizations grew weary of being forever begged and borrowed from. Still, it was an R & I department of sorts; and its mug-book library was reasonably complete in the category of career criminals. And among these last was the man following him:

August Pellino (Fat Gus, Augie the Hog); eighteen arrests, one conviction: six months. Susp. murder, extortion, narcotics, prostitution. Presumably inactive at present. Known associates, Salvatore Onate, ditto-ditto; Carlos Moroni, ditto-ditto; Victor Anglese, ditto-ditto, et cetera, et cetera.

Another bell began to ring; they were ringing all over the place tonight. Lord turned onto the highway, and then off of it, and saw happily that he was still followed.

Highlands and gangsters. Highlands and Gus Pellino.

McBride had been killed. Then Highlands' president—what was his name, Harrington?—had got it. In less than a month, two peculiar deaths right together. And Joyce had fought to get him out of town, seemingly at Pellino's urging. And now Pellino was tailing him.

Well?

Lord shrugged. He couldn't see the whole picture, only its shadowy outlines. But even those were highly revealing.

Tom Lord, for some reason, had to be gotten out of the way, and since he would not cooperate in the getting out, his exodus would have to be compelled. He couldn't be killed; at least, he couldn't be murdered. Otherwise, he would have been dead long ago. But he did have to be removed from the scene. And just how Gus Pellino planned to manage that removal, what plans he had, were a mystery.

Lord drove at as even a pace as the road would allow, grinning wryly at his occasional glances into the rear-view mirror. Pellino was keeping about a quarter-mile between them. Now and then he cut off his lights for a few minutes; seeking to give the impression, apparently, that one car turned off the road and after an interval, another turned on.

"A real smart fella," Lord murmured, chuckling. "Ought to learn me a lot when I get around to talkin' to him."

Two hours slipped by. In the moonlight's dusky darkness, they passed the abandoned wildcat where Aaron McBride had died. And Tom Lord, though not seeing it— only aware that it was off there in the loneliness to his right—ceased to smile, and the night seemed suddenly colder.

He turned on the heater.

He lighted a cigar, and took a drink from a half-pint

bottle in the glove compartment. And his eyes looked broodingly into the rear-view mirror.

It wouldn't be any trick at all to collar Pellino now. Pellino was doubtless a real handy boy around the big towns, but out here he probably stumbled over his own feet. Set a little trap for him, and he'd run over himself to get into it. Still . . .

Lord hesitated, then reluctantly shook his head. Better play it Pellino's way. Better let him run the rope out, and then see what he'd do with it.

Some ten miles past the abandoned drilling rig, Lord slowed the big convertible and switched on his spotlight. Its yellow beam jounced ball-like across the prairie, spearing a fear-struck covey of quail, glowing greenly on the saucer-size eyes of an enormous mule rabbit. A coyote, lips snarled, crouched in front of it. It flicked over a bull rattler, reared up ropishly from his hole. Then, at last, it picked out an almost indiscernible trail; two overgrown, dust-blown wheel tracks. The car turned onto them.

The shack was approximately a mile back from the road, a long, low one-room structure, with an open lean-to on its far side. Who the builder had been, Lord didn't know. Some drought-driven nester, perhaps, from pioneer days— some greenhorns had been foolish enough to attempt farming here. Or it might have served as the bunkouse for some long-ago cattle spread. As the Mexicans put it, *"Quien sabe?"* This sandy, sage-brushed vastness was a crazy quilt of mysteries. Try to trace out the threads of one, and you ran into a dozen.

Tom Lord had discovered the place years before, back when he was first coming into manhood. And gradually, through the years since then, he had made it into and maintained it as a comfortable retreat. He needed such a place—had always needed it. He needed the isolation that transcended loneliness, that gradually swung him out of the depths and up to the safety of the opposite shore.

He had never painted the exterior; and the weathered wood was part of his own background. One might pass it a hundred times, from the road, and never see it. Only a very few of his associates knew of its existence. None had visited it to his knowledge, and certainly none by his invitation.

Ordinarily, he parked his car beneath the lean-to. But tonight he stopped at the front of the shack, leaving his lights on full so that Pellino would be sure to see it.

He went into the building and lighted a lamp. Moving deliberately, frequently lazing in front of the headlights, he carried in his supplies.

He disposed of the last of them, a total of several arm-loads. Then, switching off the car lights, he re-entered the shack and slammed the door.

He mixed a drink, lighted another cigar. He smoked it down halfway, stamped it out, and blew out the lamp. He listened. A look of bewilderment spread over his face.

Pellino's car could be little more than a mile away, obscured by the growth of the roadside ditch. Lord had heard him when he cut his motor—sound traveled a long way in this chilled thin air—yet there had been no sound of the car's restarting.

What was the guy doing, anyway? Could he really be this night blind—so hard-of-seeing that he still had to assure himself of the shack's location?

Lord guessed he probably was, judging by Pellino's clumsy job of tailing. He couldn't see good himself, so he thought no one else could.

There was a push-up shutter on the lean-to side of the house. Lord raised it silently, went through the window, and crept to the corner of the building.

He had guessed right. Pellino had gotten out of the car and come up the trail on foot. He was standing two or three hundred yards away, but his white shirt—a white shirt, for Pete's sake!—was clearly visible.

Lord hesitated, then moved boldly out from the shack. Pellino obviously didn't see him, for he kept on coming. And he proceeded to advance, as Lord watched motionlessly, until he was little more than a hundred yards away. That was close enough for him, seemingly. From that distance, he could at last confirm what he had seen from the road.

He turned and started back down the trail. Grinning wickedly, Lord scooped up a handful of pebbles and followed him. He trotted, crouching, ducking low, weaving silently through green-black clumps of sagebrush. Moving at an angle to the trail, he came parallel with Pellino.

He paused there, dropping down behind a bush. Peering through its foliage, he tossed a pebble.

Pellino jumped and whirled; stood stock-still for a moment. Then he went on, and Lord continued to move after him.

His second pebble struck in front of the fat man; the third and fourth to his left and right. Each time Pellino went into a kind of startled little jig, and each time he hurried forward at a somewhat faster clip.

Lord was cautious with his tossings, making sure that Pellino only heard the pebbles without seeing them. In this way, he would doubtless accept the thumps and thuds as some ghastly local phenomenon. Something that was nerve-racking but entirely natural. For, naturally, he must not be frightened away permanently. A little fun, that was all Lord wanted. Fun for himself, and a case of nerves for Mis-ter Pellino.

The gangster scrambled into his car and drove away. Lord turned back toward the shack.

Prob'ly hadn't been very smart, he admitted, to chase around here at night; man could get himself snake-bit real easy that way. It sure hadn't been smart, and that was a fact. But it sure had been fun.

"A real entertainin' fellow," he told himself. "Plumb full of piss and high spirits. Can't hardly wait until we get t'gether again."

He grinned, and his teeth gleamed whitely in the darkness.

14

Feeling stronger than she had felt in days, Donna McBride took a hasty shower in the bathroom, her ears keyed to any sound at the door. She had propped a chair beneath the knob—there being no door key or latch—but she was still very apprehensive. Mr. Lord, her husband's friend or no, was enough to make a person nervous. Mr. Lord apparently did exactly how he pleased, and she had had one shameful sample of how he pleased.

She toweled her body, rinsed out the towel, and draped it over the tub to dry. She hastened into her underclothes, the innumerable skirts and slips, and pulled her dress over her head. With each layer of garments, she had seemed to add corresponding layers of self-assurance and primness. Fully dressed at last, she felt entirely equal to Tom Lord. She was certain of her ability to handle Lord and a half-dozen more like him.

Since his help had been thrust upon her, and in a highly embarrassing fashion, she owed him nothing. But of course she would thank him and proffer a reasonable sum in payment. She would not, however, suffer any more of his nonsense. She would not bandy words with him.

He had the answers, or he should have them, to the mystery surrounding her husband's death. He had them—something to tell her, at least—and he would give them to her. She would ask the questions, and he would provide the answers. And then she would do what she had come here to do.

She made the bed, laid the nightgown across the pillows. Her fingers lingered over it; and blushing, suddenly, she jerked her hand away and rubbed it against her dress.

She removed the chair from the door, crossed to the dresser for her purse. It was then that she saw the message lying beneath it, a single sheet of paper filled with exaggerated illiteracies.

Donna read it, and her face slowly assumed the hue of a freshly baked brick:

Sorry I cant stik around 2 C U. Hope 2 C more of U (ha-ha) when we meat agin. Help yourself to vittles, an fele free to pack a lunch. U need more meat on U, an it will probly improve your dispasistion. Also U had better not keep pickin at that itsy-bitsy mole on your rite

There were several scratchings-out at this point, the seeming results of Lord's attempts—or misattempts—to spell certain words like "breast" and "bosom." Finally, finding himself hopelessly inadequate to the task, he had drawn a tiny picture of the object in question; labelling it *R* (for right) and indicating a mole beneath the nipple.

He concluded:

Pickin' at it mite give U a infeckshun, an besides it is kind of cute. Hopping U R the same. . . .

There was no signature. In its place was a cartoon of a man waving good-bye to a woman with a suitcase in her hand. The fatuously beaming man was unmistakably Lord, and the woman—her face set in a look of preposterous rectitude—was obviously intended as Donna McBride. She wore a Russian shako, earmuffs, overshoes, a blanket-size scarf, and enormous fur gloves. Her body was so voluminously clothed that she appeared practically as wide as she was tall.

Donna wadded the revolting document and hurled it to the floor. Then, with angry reluctance, she snatched it up and examined it again. Her color deepened. Unconsciously, her hands strayed over her body, tested the quiltlike volume of her clothing. Unwillingly, she stole a glance at herself in the mirror.

Did she really look like the woman in the cartoon? Was there actually any resemblance between her own expression and the one worn by *that* ridiculous creature?

The questions weren't worth answering, she decided. She would not dignify them with her interest. She looked as she should look, as a decent, self-respecting woman. And if people thought there was something funny about that, why—why——

She threw the paper to the floor again, and stamped on it. Then, having made sure that Lord was not hiding on the premises, she left the house.

It was still quite early in the morning, but people arose early out here, and the sheriff and several deputies were already on duty. As Donna paused in the office doorway, stood there looking about her sternly, the deputies arose with elaborate casualness and lounged into an adjoining room. Donna turned a severe gaze on the sheriff. And to her surprise, he gave her a smile of welcome.

" 'Mornin', Miz McBride. Lookin' mighty purt' this mornin'. Have yourself a chair."

"Why—why, thank you . . ." She sat down gingerly, wondering at his change in attitude. "Thank you very much, Sheriff Bradley."

She sat very straight, hands folded in her lap, knees pressed closely together, her dress pulled over her ankles. With the innocent license of the elderly, Bradley examined her from head to foot and emitted a grunt of approval.

"You're a nice young lady, Miz McBride. Sorry if I didn't act too friendly yesterday."

"It's quite all right. Now——"

"Yessir, a real little lady, Miz McBride, an' don't you let no one tell you different. Not like these painted-up, bob-tailed fillies y' see chasin' around out here. All sass and short skirts. You know what, Miz McBride? If I was the

pa of some of them girls, I'd just naturally cut me a switch
an' . . ."

He rambled on, and Donna, after a few attempts to cut
in, lapsed into sympathetic silence. Age was entitled to
respect. And this man, with his occasionally cracking voice,
his occasional high-pitched cackle, his advanced senility,
was entitled to much more: to kindness, to a feeling of
being important, to patience, to all the things so often
denied a man when his need for them is greatest.

The aimless rambling came to faltering end. He sighed
heavily and returned to the present.

"Well, let's see, now. Uh, what was it that—uh——?"

"Tom Lord, Sheriff. Could you please tell me where he
is?"

"Ain't t'his his house? Big place up on the hill, with a
doctor's sign on it."

"He's not there, no."

"Uh-*hah*," Bradley drawled, stroking his chin. "Well,
that figgers. Prob'ly thought it'd be healthier out of town
for a while."

"Yes?" Donna frowned. "I don't understand, Sheriff."

"Sure, you don't," he nodded emphatically, "because I
didn't say nothin', did I? Sure didn't say he'd be dodgin'
a nice little lady like you."

"But, Sheriff. I"—she caught herself and made an effort
to return Bradley's knowing smile. He was obviously skirt-
ing a dangerous subject. If he told her anything, it would
be only because of his certainty that she already knew it.

"No," she smiled, "you haven't said a word, Sheriff. But just to make sure that we understand each other, why don't you *not* say something more?"

"Now, I'll just do that, Miz McBride," he cackled in shrill appreciation. "I'll just not say nothing about what you got in your purse. Nothin' at all—even if it has got a certain swing to it which an old hand like me can spot a mile off, and even if it does fall a certain way when you set it down, and even if . . ."

Donna listened to him, confused at first, wondering what the gun had to do with Tom Lord; and then, as the apparent truth began to dawn on her, a faint sickish feeling and a strange sense of loss came over her. It was difficult to believe that Lord, irritating and insulting as he was, could commit murder. After all—though he'd certainly been very rude!— Lord had ministered to her gently and obviously quite ably. She'd been seriously ill, perhaps dangerously so, she realized now, and Lord had——

She sucked in her breath sharply. Never mind those things! He, Lord, had killed her husband. Bradley was sure that he had, just as he was sure that she intended to kill Lord.

Which was exactly what she was going to do!

Still. . . .

"Sheriff Bradley," she said, "is there some reason why— can't he be tried and convicted?"

"Wouldn't be runnin' loose if he could ma'am. Ain't got a smidgeon of proof, and that's a fact."

"But you're sure? There's no doubt in your mind?"

"Well, sure I'm sure." He squinted at her dubiously. "Ain't you?"

Donna said quickly that she was. She had simply wanted to confirm her opinion.

"Where is he, Sheriff Bradley?"

"Now, ma'am." He shook his head with slow firmness. "You know I can't do that. Got all the sympathy in the world for you, but I can't help you take the law into your own hands. Stuck my neck out a long ways as it is."

"Please. No one will ever know that you told me."

"I'd know." A slight frostiness came into his eyes. "Fact is, I ain't absolutely positive where he is, anyhow. It's just a hunch."

"But——"

"Maybe you just better forget it. Leave Tom to us. He'll get took care of one way or another."

He nodded with cool politeness, turned around to his desk. It was final. He would say nothing more.

Donna left, started down the corridor to the stairs. As she approached, a tall, lean man raised his head from the drinking fountain. A pearl-handled pistol hung from his bullet-studded gun belt. His eyes and nose were badly swollen, and his protruding lips were bruised and puffy.

He ducked his head as she swerved toward him, quickly putting his hand to his mouth.

"Tom Lord murdered my husband," she said firmly. "I think you know it, and I think you know where he can be found. Now, I insist that you tell me."

"Sure wish I could, ma'am." He kept his head ducked, his hand up. "Right sorry."

"You've got to! How can you refuse to help me, when you won't do anything yourselves?"

"You leave Tom to us, ma'am. He'll get took care of, one way or another."

He brushed past her, heading for the sheriff's office. Frowning thoughtfully, Donna started down the stairs.

"Leave Tom to us. Get took care of one way or another...."

Both Bradley and the puffy-mouthed man had said the same thing. Or practically the same thing. And they had said it so positively, as though they were giving her their solemn promise. Still, if they did really mean it, if it wasn't just a manner of speaking, why couldn't they tell her more—give her some proof of their good faith? Some hint as to just how and when Lord would be taken care of. Why all this caution with her, the party most concerned?

It was probably just talk, she decided bitterly. Just bluster. They might want to see Lord punished, but they would do nothing to bring that punishment about. If they had meant to, they would have done it before this.

As she emerged from the courthouse and into the brilliant sunlight, a wave of weakness swept over her, and she remembered that she had had nothing to eat since the previous evening's light repast. She weaved slightly, biting her lip. She tottered to a nearby tree, and braced herself against it. Slowly, the weakness and the darkness retreated.

They were not completely gone, however. She could feel their nearness, sense their hovering presence in every fiber of her body.

Cautiously, carefully putting one foot in front of the other, she headed for the railroad station. There was a dining room there. Her baggage was checked there, too, and perhaps she had best decide what to do about it. She had not taken a hotel room the day before, her plans being uncertain (as, of course, they still were). Moreover, hotels were expensive, and she had a very limited amount of money.

Her hospital and doctor bills had been huge. Equally huge—far more so, in fact—was the expense of two funerals. Aaron and the baby had had the very best that could be had, with no thought of economy, and she was fiercely glad and proud of giving it to them. But the house, put up for a forced fast sale, had brought only a fraction of its value, and when all the bills were paid, there had been practically nothing left of the proceeds.

Aside from a modest checking account, McBride had left no other estate. He had always drawn a good salary. He had also, however, always had the double expense of maintaining himself in the field as well as a home in Fort Worth. And then there had been the bills from his first wife's long illness.

His death was not covered by the mandatory workmen's insurance. As for other insurance, he had none, such being against his principles. She had once suggested, before she was aware of his attitude, that he take out a policy. He didn't really get angry about it, but she was made to feel exceedingly uncomfortable.

He gave her a good living, he pointed out—everything that she needed, within reason. His health being excellent, he should continue to do so indefinitely, until he was overtaken by old age. By which time, naturally, he would have accumulated more than enough for comfortable retirement. And if he didn't, if some misfortune should alter this schedule, Donna would be quite young enough to go to work.

"As you should," he said steadily, "if you had any real or lasting regard for me. I've seen too many of these insurance widows. They don't stay widows long if they've got any money. The first husband skimps and slaves to pay for the insurance, and then some slick-haired gigolo of a second husband comes along and lives high on the proceeds."

Donna could understand his feelings. In a terrible vision, she saw herself lolling about the house (drugged, perhaps, or under some strange hypnotic spell), looking on helplessly while a villain in evening clothes opened endless bottles of champagne and lighted five-dollar cigars with hundred-dollar bills.

Aaron was right. Aaron was always right; a kindly and all-wise man, protecting her from her own ignorance. The fact that he had left her practically penniless was Lord's fault, and his alone.

She entered the railroad station, paused before the door

which led to the connecting dining room. A menu was pasted to the glass, and she examined it with a feeling of horror.

Twenty-five cents for a cup of coffee! *Twenty-five* cents! Ham-and-egg breakfast, *two dollars and fifty cents*. Special budget breakfast, *one dollar and sixty cents*. Orange juice . . .

Almost reeling, Donna mentally counted the money in her purse. She had assumed, naturally, that prices might be a little high here. It was a boom area, and consumer goods would have to be shipped in from great distances. But this! *These* prices!

She supposed she would have to eat a little something. But just how was she going to manage for more than a very few days. . . .

"My name is Howard," said a voice at her side. "Will you join me for breakfast?"

Donna whirled around, eyes automatically icing over, her face setting itself in severely forbidding lines. And then seeing the man—the sandy grey hair, the broad, honest face, the stout, stodgy body—she relaxed. She even smiled a little.

"Well, I . . . I'm afraid I don't know you, Mr. Howard."

"I'm sorry. I knew your husband very well. He spoke to me about you many times, and I assumed he'd mentioned me to you."

He was obviously a little hurt, and she hastened to make amends. "I'm sure he must have, Mr. Howard. It's just that I've been so upset, and——"

"Of course you have. You've had every right to be. When I think of that miserable creature Lord!" He shook his head in angry sympathy. "If I was only a little younger, I'd go out to that shack of his and——"

"Shack!" She gripped his arm excitedly. "Do you know where it is, Mr. Howard? Could you take me there?"

"Why, yes. Of course. But"—he gave her a grave look—"I'm by no means sure that I should. I'm afraid I spoke a little impulsively a moment ago. I certainly didn't mean to imply that you should, uh. . . ."

"Who else is there? Please, Mr. Howard," she begged. "You know what a fine man Aaron was. You know that nothing will be done about his murder, unless I do it!"

Howard nodded, but he would not commit himself. He was completely in accord with her. In her position, he was confident that his own daughter would feel exactly as she did. Still it was a very serious matter, this taking of the law into one's own hands, and not one to be rushed into hastily.

"We shall see," he said, pushing open the door to the dining room. "We'll talk about it while we eat."

He nodded firmly as she hesitated, a man determined to take no drastic step without due deliberation.

So Donna went through the door. And Howard, otherwise Gus Pellino, trudged after her.

15

On their long ride out into the wilderness, Donna began to have some second thoughts about her mission, to doubt its rightness and her wisdom. She had been swept along so rapidly—or, rather, she had driven herself along so rapidly,—that there had been no time to think. But now she began to see the contradictions, or apparent ones, between Lord as he was—the man she had met—and the allegedly murderous Lord.

Clearly, Tom Lord was a highly intelligent man; he was, had to be, despite his yokel's masquerade. It would not be like him to kill another so clumsily as to incriminate himself. Then, and again despite the masquerade, Lord was a man of breeding, a man of family. She could picture him killing in a fight—a duel, if duels were still fought. But . . . but murder?

He was no friend of Aaron's. For doubtless very good reasons. Aaron had not told the truth about that. But while they were not friends, Aaron had had no fear of him. And Aaron, invariably shrewd as he was, would have immediately seen the danger—and taken proper precautions against it—if Lord had presented any.

It came to Donna suddenly that her suspicions of murder were not based on incontrovertible evidence. All the suspicious circumstances could have been explained away by anyone with any claim to cleverness—Lord, for example. Instead, however, no one would tell her anything. There was only the rather stupid theory that Aaron had taken his own life. And when she tried to probe beyond that, she ran into a wall of silence.

Was this proof of murder? Did Bradley and his lanky deputy *know* that Lord had murdered her husband, or was there another reason for the animosity toward him?

She slid an uneasy glance toward her companion; hesitated on the point of addressing him.

He had tried to talk her out of this. She had had to beg, plead, argue—point out his duty to him as Aaron's good friend—before he finally assented to it. Now, they were out here, some seventy miles in the country; almost to Tom Lord's hideaway. They were here at her insistence and against his, Howard's, wishes. So just how, without looking like a complete ninny, could she suggest that——

"By the way," said Pellino casually, "have you ever seen Lord? Without knowing who he was, I mean."

"Well, yes, I have. I thought he was a doctor."

"I see," said Pellino, and he did seem to see something; to rid himself of a minor puzzle. "As a matter of fact, I believe he did practically qualify as a doctor. Too shiftless and lazy, apparently, to take his degree."

"Mr. Howard, I—I just wonder if——"

"Strange," Pellino continued soberly, "strange how a man with every possible advantage—a fine family, an excellent education, amazing good looks—could turn out as he has. Didn't you think he was strikingly handsome, Mrs. McBride? Why, if he had a spark of decency or ambition, he could be a big-time movie star!"

Donna nodded uncomfortably. Somehow or other, the words she had been about to say to Mr. Howard seemed suddenly awkward. Even a little shameful.

"Do you know something, Mrs. McBride?" Pellino smiled apologetically. "Do you know the real reason why I hesitated about bringing you out here today?"

"Well"—Donna braced herself—"I suppose you thought I was being a little headstrong and foolish . . ."

"I was afraid you'd back out at the last moment. Lord is quite a lady's man, you know. They get very angry with him at times—with good reason, I might add. But when it gets down to taking any action against him, well, that's something else again."

Donna swallowed. Laughed nervously. She was about to say that whatever she did or didn't do would certainly have nothing to do with Lord's alleged charm and good looks. But Pellino was again ahead of her.

"You see, Mrs. McBride, I'd heard a bit of gossip around town. Lord always talks about his conquests, naturally, and with the two of you alone in the house together, why . . ."

"B-but—*conquests!*" Donna's face flamed furiously.

"B-but I told you! I didn't know who he was! I thought he was a doctor, and——"

"Of course. Of course, you did. You don't have to convince me, Mrs. McBride. I know that Aaron's wife wouldn't have an affair with his murderer."

"Or with anyone else!"

Pellino murmured vaguely. He said that she must do exactly as she wished, with no thought to his own old-fashioned notions. "You mustn't mind me, Mrs. McBride. Just say the word and I'll turn around and drive you back to town. I might be disappointed, but believe me, I can understand how an attractive young woman like you, and a man as handsome as Lord could—uh——"

He broke off, the insinuating words seemingly rammed down his throat by Donna's look.

"I'm sorry," he mumbled apologetically. "I just wanted you to be sure."

"Well, I am sure, and you can be sure, too! Now, aren't we about there?"

"Why, yes," said Pellino, and he brought the car to a stop. "Here's the trail right here."

She climbed out, stumbled awkwardly as she literally plunged across the roadside ditch. Then, without a look backward, she went on up the trail; head high, back very straight.

Pellino chuckled fatly, and congratulated himself. He'd managed the thing perfectly; let her talk herself into the hole, and then slammed the lid on it. She'd never back down now. As steamed up as she was, she could probably take Lord apart with her bare hands. And if it shouldn't work out that way, if the situation was reversed and she became Lord's victim, well, that would be all right, too. A slight switch of plans and the result would be the same.

Pellino turned the car around and drove away.

Donna came nearer the shack, her footsteps remaining firm, her purpose unshaken. When she stopped at last, some fifty feet away from the building, it was only to rest and reconnoiter.

She patted her face with her handkerchief. She looked around her, fighting to ignore the loneliness, the desolation that seemed to creep forward steathily. Somewhere a twig snapped. She whirled, startled, and from behind her came another sound; a cactus pod falling to the ground. She jerked her head this way and that, to the front, the side, the rear. And the wind whined like a hungry thing; it opened a thousand little paths for the stalking loneliness, then hastily closed the paths over.

Well—Donna gave herself a little shake—well, so she was alone. Lord's car was nowhere in sight, so apparently he was away, and she was alone. And what of it? Mr. Howard would wait for her indefinitely. Nothing was changed. There was nothing to get alarmed about.

She pounded on the door. She tested it, found it unlocked, and went in.

There was a table and a few chairs, a huge kerosene refrigerator-freezer, and a medium-sized kerosene range. Two long shelves angled halfway around the room; stacked with books mostly, but also holding a small radio, several boxes of rifle shells, a doctor's medicine kit, and various other items. The bed was a crude, knocked-together bunk, but it had a box-spring mattress.

Tom Lord, obviously, liked to rough it in comfort. Donna sniffed disapprovingly, and sat down to wait for him.

About a half-hour had passed when she heard his car approaching. Edging back one of the scrim window curtains, she looked out.

He wasn't coming up the trail, but across the prairie, riding along a ridgeback of rock to the rear of the house. He was scrounged down comfortably in the seat, one leg hung over the door. His Stetson was pushed back on his head, and a cigar was cocked in his mouth.

Donna's lips pressed together. That he should carry on like this, utterly carefree, with poor Aaron so soon in his grave!

She took the gun from her purse, checked the chamber. She flung the door open and stepped through it.

He had to see her, of course, as he jounced up the slope toward the house. But he gave no sign of the fact. He ran the car under the lean-to, clambered out lazily with a rifle cradled under his arm. Then, as he turned toward the door of the shack, he at last took note of her presence. Falling back in exaggerated surprise, he swept off his hat with a flourish.

"Now, don't tell me, ma'am," he smirked. "I'll think of it in a minute. Face looks awful familiar, but I don't quite place the body."

"Mr. Lord," Donna snapped. "You know quite well who

I am, and you must know why I'm here. I am going to kill you."

"Well, there ain't no point in bein' cross about it," Lord said. "You just come right on in an' get yourself set, and I'll cook us some steak an' smashed pertaters."

"I'm quite serious, Mr. Lord!"

"An' you think I'm jokin'? Well, you just wait and see. Might even whip up some batter biscuits an' cream gravy."

He waved her ahead of him, adding a firm push to the gesture. Then, righting her as she stumbled across the threshold, he handed her the rifle.

"Mind puttin' this up on them pegs?" He nodded toward the wall. "I'll be diggin' us out some meat."

He went over to the refrigerator. Bending from the waist, his pants drawn tight across his buttocks, he peered into the freezer bin.

Donna almost moaned in fury, looked helplessly from the rifle in one hand to the pistol in the other. Her hat had slipped over one eye when he pushed her. And now a wisp of hair fell down across her nose. She blew upward on it, eyes turned in to watch the result. Blindly, she poked and probed with the barrel of the rifle; and the muzzle hooked in the crown of her hat and the hat rose neatly from her head.

So she stood, eyes rolled in, hat held aloft like a standard. Lord withdrew his head from the freezer and looked at her between his legs.

"You don't look very comfortable, ma'am. Like me t' get you a drink of water or somethin'?"

Donna groaned. She hurled the rifle to the bed, the hat sailing along with it, and slapped the hair from her eyes.

"Y-you!" she stammered. "Y-you—you—you! Do you hear me, Tom Lord? I'm going to kill you!"

"Oh, yeah," said Lord. "Guess you did say somethin' like that, didn't you?"

"You stand up!"

"What for?" He reached up and patted his rump. "Got yourself a better target this way."

"Y-you—you stand up!"

"Well, okay." He straightened himself lazily. "But it's gonna hold up our dinner. Now, how you want me—front view or profile?"

Donna ignored the question. Hand suddenly steady, she took aim at his chest. "I am a very good shot with this, Mr. Lord," she said evenly. And she was a good shot: she had practiced for this moment. "Now, if you have anything to say for yourself, any excuse for killing my husband, you'd better speak quickly."

"Can't think of a thing," Lord said. "Reckon I just got primed up to kill someone, so I done it."

"That . . . that's all you have to say? Y-you just——"

"Well, you know how it is." An edge came into his voice. "Seems like you ought to, anyways. Got your mind made up to kill someone, you don't need no excuse."

"I see," said Donna grimly. "I see."

She pulled the trigger.

She kept pulling it, and Lord pitched to the floor with an agonized scream.

He threshed about wildly, writhing in the death throes, his screams still ripping from his lips. And then suddenly, with a violent shuddering gasp, he was silent. Completely silent. He was still. Completely still.

The gun dropped from Donna's fingers. She stared at him, eyes growing wider and wider, and from what seemed a great distance she heard a voice. Her own voice:

"No," she said. *"Oh, no, no, no, no. . . ."*

She shoked on a great sob. She sank down on her knees by the still body and buried her face in her hands.

Why? she asked herself. *How could I? I knew he didn't do it. I KNEW IT! But I lost my temper, and . . . and Mr. Howard . . . he . . . he . . .*

But why? Where the reason for this terrible deed? She had demanded a reason of him, his excuse for a crime of which he was guiltless. Now, she *had* done this, and what was her reason?

She wept in bewildered terror. "Why?" she sobbed aloud.

"Oh, God, why did I do it?"

"Now, I'll ask you one," said Tom Lord. "Why did the chicken cross the road?"

She gasped; slowly took her hands from her face. Lord drew his shirt open, revealing his broad, unmarked chest.

"Look, Mom," he said. "No holes."

16

Gus Pellino slowed his car and turned up the trail to the abandoned drilling well. He had set no definite time for picking Donna up. Obviously, he could not have, since there was no way of knowing whether Lord was away from his shack or how long he might be gone. So he had told her simply to wait for him—either in the shack or its vicinity—implying that he would somehow manage to arrive immediately after her mission was accomplished. Actually, he did not intend to return until well after dark.

He hadn't got a good look at his surroundings last night. He'd been far too busy watching the road and keeping an eye on Lord. Today, however, he'd quickly seen the danger in the terrain; noted the distance that almost any sizable object could be observed. And he knew he must not loiter in the open for long.

He'd gotten all the breaks thus far, passing no one on the road out from town or on his way back to the well. Except for Lord, then, the only person living in the area, no one could have seen his car. And if Lord had seen it from his shack, it didn't really matter. For the ex-deputy was as good as dead.

Lord would take no decisive action against the girl. Aside from foolish considerations of chivalry, he couldn't do it, and the fact that he couldn't was apparent in his flight out here from Big Sands.

Rough up a woman? Stand up to her in a showdown—the widow of the man you'd killed?

Huh-uh. They'd throw the book at you, no matter how right you were or how wrong she was.

Lord's only chance had been to run away from her, to hide out until she gave up and quit. That hadn't worked, and now he was a dead man or soon would be.

Pellino parked his car behind the bunkhouse. He got out, yawned and stretched lazily, and looked around him. There wasn't much to see. Just more of the same, with minor variations, that he'd been seeing.

The land sloped downward gently, clustered with the usual rock outcroppings, cacti, and sagebrush. Then, as the slope sharpened, it became wooded, gnarled blackjack trees thrusting up from the rocky and shallow soil. And finally the trees became so thick as to obscure all else.

Pellino noted the weathered framework of a building, and he shook his head cynically. McBride's house, or house-to-be. Virtuously, he'd filed itemized reports of his use of company materials—and he'd been docked plenty for them! And now the stupid sap was dead.

How dumb could you get, anyway, Pellino wondered. Why, a smart guy could have knocked down twenty grand a year on the company, and no one would have been the wiser! Just grab a little here and a little there, and you'd have it made. Yet this cluck McBride hadn't left his widow a pot to toss it out of.

Well . . . something brushed against Pellino's cheek and he slapped at it absently . . . well, to hell with McBride and his widow, too. She'd be as dead as he was before long. She had to be to complete the picture that someone would discover, weeks or perhaps even months from now.

Lord with his tail shot off . . . the girl beaten to death.

She'd wounded him mortally, he'd injured her fatally. They'd killed each other, see, and the setup was such that they logically could have done that. There wasn't a chance of a kickback; no more, at any rate, than the ever-present one-in-a-million chance. By the time someone did get around to stopping by the shack—something which no one had any reason to do—it would be impossible to dope out the approximate time of the two deaths. Impossible to say that the girl had died hours later than the man. Or if such was possible, well, what the hell did it prove? They could have died at widely separate times from injuries incurred at about the same time.

Pellino doubled his heavy fists, flexed the bunched muscles of his arms. It would be good to have a little real action again. There was nothing like heavy work for keeping a man in shape. With a dame, of course, you hardly had a chance to get up a sweat. But there were compensations for the dearth of exercise.

After all, there was more than one kind of exercise, just as there was more than one kind of sweating. And no one knew it better than Gus Pellino.

Thinking of Donna and his plans for her, his thoughts drifted automatically to his wife. And the lewd smile on his face changed to a frown.

He called his wife each night at six o'clock and gave her a seemingly innocuous coded report of the day's happenings, plus his plans—insofar as he knew them—for the next day. His wife passed the report on to his associates. As long as he reported, all was presumed to be well with him. If he failed to—exactly at six o'clock—an opposite assumption would be made. And it would be far later than six before he could report tonight.

"Goddamn!" Gus scowled. "Now, what the hell . . . ?"

His associates knew of his plans only in the most general way. Necessarily so, since most of them had been made after six last night. And if there should be a foul-up, they would have only the vaguest idea of where he was or what to do about it.

Pellino cursed viciously. There would be no foul-up, of course. The deal was in the bag, and the bag had no holes. But still, a thing like this wasn't good. It would hurt him, even though he checked in the minute he hit town. By that time, the boys would have gotten jumpy. They might even go to the point of swinging into action. He'd have pulled them out of the soup, naturally, and that was all to the good. But they'd still be irritated with him. Unavoidably or not, he'd 've put them on a spot where they could have been left high and dry. And a thing like that you didn't live down in a hurry.

Pellino brushed at his face again. Another one of those goddamned bugs, or something. They'd been doing it last night, zipping past him and plinking down around him, making him jump and look around in spite of himself. And they were at it fullforce today. But they didn't bother him now. He wouldn't let them. Had enough on his mind without worrying about a bunch of stinking bugs or grasshoppers . . . or whatever the hell they were. They'd gotten him kind of jumpy last night, but that was in the dark. Today, when he could see there was no one around, when he knew there couldn't be anyone——

There was a small sound behind him. Angrily, he ignored it.

Then something jabbed into his spine, a something that could only be a gun, and a drawling voice addressed him:

"Don't turn around, mister. First time you do, it'll be the last."

Pellino nodded jerkily. Guns he didn't argue with. It was Lord; it had to be. And talking, rather than action, was in order.

"Looks like I stubbed my toe, Lord," he said, his mouth very dry, "but maybe we're going the same way. You play along with me, and I'll give you a deal that——"

"Reckon I'll do my own dealin', mister. Kind of come out better that way with me holding the aces."

"Not all of them, Lord. Let me show you my hand."

"Show me the way down to that toolhouse," the voice advised him. "Just follow that big nose of yours, an' it'll lead you to it."

"But, listen, Lord. . . ."

"Stop talkin' and start walkin' "—the gun, a rifle apparently, jabbed painfully—"just keep followin' your nose, or you won't have no head to wear it on."

Pellino obeyed. The rifleman—Lord, naturally; it had to be Lord—meant what he said.

Hands half-raised, he moved toward the open door of the toolhouse. The rifle continued to press against his back, its owner almost treading on his heels. Yet despite his predicament—the outrageous fate that had placed him here—he was not badly frightened, nor by any means hopeless.

Lord didn't mean to kill him; not in the immediate future at any rate. If he had meant to, he could've done it back there behind the bunkhouse. So seemingly—and at Lord's convenience—they were destined to have a talk. And when it came to talking, Gus Pellino could . . .

His heart skipped a beat, a sickish feeling coming into his stomach, as he saw the high-banked oval abutting the well. The slush-pit! He knew enough about the oil racket to identify it—a small, man-made lake, filled with the oozing mud from the well.

Was this why he hadn't been killed immediately? Was Lord marching him down here toward the pit, so that he . . . ?

But, no—he began to breathe again—no, he was continuing on toward the toolhouse. Going straight ahead instead of to the side. And now he was stepping up on the loading platform, approaching the dark doorway.

The rifle suddenly came away from his back. Something smashed against his head, and he pitched forward through the door.

He was out only a few minutes, or what seemed only a few minutes. Head throbbing, he came shakily to his feet, squinted about the toolshed's shadowy interior. The door was closed tightly—barred, he guessed, after leaning his weight against it. He patted his pockets, and emitted a grunt of surprise.

This didn't add up. Lord rolling him for his wallet. Lord wouldn't mess around with mere robbery. So maybe it wasn't Lord, huh? Maybe . . .

But, no, it had to be. Had to, because it just couldn't be anyone else. Lord wasn't after his dough, of course. He was looking for information—something incriminating. And a hell of a lot of good it would do him. Gus Pellino was no sap, even though he momentarily appeared to be. A few bucks in cash, a few receipts for bills paid, a couple of credit cards—that would be about the size of Lord's findings.

Pellino listened, holding his ear to the door. He circled

the walls, listening, peering through the tiny cracks between the boards.

He could see nothing and hear nothing; nothing, at least,
to indicate that Lord was around. But that didn't mean—
Gus remembered grimly—that he *wasn't*. The guy was like
a lousy cat. Sneak right up on you and tease you while he
was doing it.

Pellino tested the door again. He braced his shoulder
against it, pushing with his legs, and the door bulged slowly
outward. A little bit more and he'd snap those bars like
matchsticks.

But hell—he stood back from it suddenly—that
wouldn't do. He'd be *expected* to crash out the door. That
side of the building would be watched, if there was anyone
around to watch. Any getting out would have to be done
on the other side, and with a minimum of noise.

His eyes were becoming adjusted to the dimness now,
and he could see reasonably well. The heavy planking of
the walls (*need a sledge-hammer to smash through them*).
The grimy floors, splintered here and there where some
heavy object had been dropped. Some greasy work clothes,
piled in a corner. Pellino raked the pile with his foot, and
uncovered a rusted object with a hook at one end. He
snatched it up, chuckling in ugly triumph.

A crowbar! Now, wasn't that nice? Wasn't that thoughtful of Lord to leave him a crowbar?

He went down on his knees, jammed the flattened end
of the bar between two floorboards, and pried cautiously

but firmly upward. He loosened them quickly, then loosened two others. Using his bare hands, working in virtual silence, he pulled them free of the floor. For this was the best way out, the only logical way. The shed sat up on a high foundation, so that its floor was high, to facilitate the loading and unloading of trucks. There was plenty of room for a man to crawl under it—even a man like Gus Pellino—and on out from beneath the rear of the building. At least, there appeared to be plenty of room. Any native of the area would have known that there might not be, that any covered-over place—even the space beneath a fallen tree—was apt to have other tenants: Golden-skinned creatures with sinuous, diamond-patterned bodies.

It was not an extraordinarily populous den for this region. During the periodic rattlesnake drives, some dens of two and three hundred had been found; and the one that Gus Pellino crawled into held only a few dozen. But that was still a great many—even one can be a great many. And the majority of these were young, their venom at its deadliest.

Pellino struggled back through the floorboards, eyes fixed and bulging, teeth bared in the hideously insensible grin of absolute shock. A huge bull, jaws locked in a death grip, dangled from his nose. Others swung from his ears and throat and shoulders. Little ones—infants and youngsters—swarmed up his pants legs and under his shirt; raced over his body in squirming, angry tangles.

Pellino clawed and struck at them. He flailed at them with numbing arms, and his grin widened, almost stretching from ear to ear; and a bubbling scream vomited from his mouth.

"Eeeeeeeee-Yah! Eeeeee-YAHH-ah-ah-a-hhhh . . ."

It was over almost as soon as it began. In a bare two minutes, he was dead, his body already swelling with poison.

17

Donna McBride awakened about mid-morning, yawned and stretched lazily; and then sat up with a sudden start. Then, remembering, she sank back down on the bunk; glanced doubtfully at the knocked-together bolster which divided the bed.

She hadn't approved of this arrangement at all. But the bolster did make it all right, she supposed. Or almost all right. She'd kept her clothes on. He'd kept his on, or most of them, she guessed. So everything was probably proper enough; and, anyway, she'd had no choice but to accept.

"Now, looky," Lord had drawled. "You're satisfied I ain't a murderer, right? Maybe I acted pretty stupid. Maybe I was looking for trouble. But I sure didn't commit murder."

"Oh, yes. I know you didn't," she said eagerly. "I'm so ashamed of myself, and I'm so grateful to you for——"

"No trouble at all. Just a matter of unloadin' your gun while you slept, taking the lead out of the bullets, and reloadin' it. Y'might say," he grinned, "that I was more than glad to do it."

"And I'm glad you did! But, Mr. Lord, I don't see what——"

"No, I reckon you don't. You wouldn't see it. A fella doctors you up, puts you on your feet, an' you try to kill him. He straightens you out, keeps you from bein' a murderer, and doctors you again. Then he gives you the best meal you ever had in your life, an'——"

"I'm well aware of your kindness! I've tried to express my gratitude."

"I don't want it. All I want is half of my own bed. Now, do I get it or do you get the whole thing?"

"Well. I suppose if you put it that way . . ."

"Now, you're talkin'," said Lord. "Nothin' I like better than a appreciative and considerate guest."

Well, that was the way it happened. But it would not happen again. He had left the shack while she slept, taking his rifle with him. Presumably he was off shooting snakes, as he had been yesterday ("My only vice, ma'am"). But as soon as he returned, she would leave.

She had to. He'd doubtless be glad to drive her into town, or to do anything else, if it meant getting rid of her.

She climbed out of the bunk, ruefully examining her slept-in clothes. She saw the piece of paper propped up on the table, and apprehensively she picked it up. But it was nothing like his first message to her. She read it, fighting back a smile, telling herself that it was really rather vulgar and therefore not to be smiled at:

We have no indoor plumbing. In using the exterior facilities (courtesy of Mother Nature) please examine the terrain very carefully. You might drown a snake.

Donna made her face prim. She left the shack, taking the paper with her. She returned without it, after a few minutes, and set the coffee on to warm. She washed in the enamel basin, again frowningly examined her dress.

It would have to hang out, she decided; she'd have to get rid of at least a few of the wrinkles. And these under-things—they'd simply have to have a quick rinse.

She got out of the garments hastily. She grabbed a pair of Lord's jeans and a shirt down from a wall peg, and quickly clambered into them. They were far too big of course, despite her tuckings and turnings, but they made her feel much less of a mess. During the brief time she would spend with Lord, she would feel much more comfortable.

She spread the dress over some bushes. Having rinsed out the underthings, she similarly disposed of them. Her hair needed a lot done to it, and there was little that she could do, and she would have welcomed a bath. But, well, how could a woman keep herself fixed up in a place like this? Lord somehow seemed to be immaculate. She had never seen anyone so utterly clean. His nails; his hair, the scrubbed scalp showing at the part; his teeth—everything about him gleamed and glistened with cleanliness. And doubtless he thought she was a frump, and a soiled one at that. But she just couldn't help it.

Aaron—poor, poor Aaron—had been a little careless

about his person. He had cited the almost primitive conditions under which he lived in the oil fields; pointed out that he could hardly change the habits acquired there on his visits home. But Lord was surrounded by the same conditions—they were even more primitive here—and yet he . . .

She heard his car in the distance. Jumping up from the table, she ran to the wavy mirror again; gave herself some frantic last-minute pats and pushes and pullings. The results, in her own mind, were wholly unsatisfactory. She looked worse than she had before. She started to redo the redoings, and her fingers fumbled and got in one another's way. And, angrily, hearing the car door slam, she gave up. So all right! She looked like h-e-double-l. She just didn't give a darn, and to heck with what Tom Lord thought of her!

He came in. He nodded politely and gave her hand a cordial shake. Addressing her as "mister" (he was plumb glad to make her acquaintance), he asked if she had seen anything of a big pile of clothes with a little gal in the middle of 'em.

Donna smirked nervously, suddenly laughed out loud. Lord grinned, his eyes approving as they moved over her.

"Look real sassy, ma'am. How'd you sleep last night?"

"Very well, thank you. All things considered, that is. I mean, I would have slept well if, uh——"

"Uh-huh," said Lord sympathetically. "I bet I woke you up with all that huggin' and kissin'."

"Hugging and kiss——!" Donna caught herself. "Mr. Lord, I'll have to ask a favor of you."

Lord nodded absently and opened the refrigerator. Donna hesitated, decided to delay her request to be driven into town. Lord obviously wanted his lunch. Also, her clothes had not yet dried.

He emerged from the refrigerator with prepared biscuits and a cardboard tray of chicken. He accepted Donna's offer of assistance, directing her to make fresh coffee and set the table.

She got busy. They brushed together occasionally as they worked, and Donna felt a fearful tingling at each contact. She fled from it, tried to dispel the too-companionable silence with a flurry of talk.

Wasn't there quite a lot of wild game in this area? Didn't he ever shoot any of it?

Lord said that he would much prefer to shoot people, there being quite a lot of them, too, and their meat being wholly unavailable in the local markets.

Donna said that didn't sound very nice. Lord said that shooting helpless animals didn't sound very nice to him. Then, seeing her expression, he sighed and rolled his eyes heavenward.

"Look," he said. "That was a j-o-a-k, joke. Do you really think I go around huntin' people?"

"Oh, no. No, of course not. I—what do you suppose happened to Mr. How—to Pellino?"

"I didn't shoot him, if that's what you mean."

"I just wondered. The way you talked yesterday, about what his plans probably were, why I——"

"Must've had to change 'em," Lord said. "Or maybe

someone changed them for him. Fella like that probably ain't real popular."

"Y-you—you think someone may have killed him?"

"Or scared him into runnin'. Anyway, he didn't pay us a visit yesterday, so he ain't likely to." Lord opened the oven door, looked in at the browning biscuits. "Don't you worry about him or anyone else. I keep an eye on the road when I'm off shootin'. Can't no one come this way without me seein' 'em."

Donna nodded. She started to say that she would not be worried, in any case, since her stay was about to end. But again the time seemed inappropriate.

Lord dished up the food. Donna said she really wasn't hungry—after all, she'd just finished breakfast. And Lord said he sympathized with her, but he never ate by himself and he had no intention of beginning now.

He seemed very serious about it (although, of course, he couldn't be). So Donna, who *was* hungry, strangely enough, did away with half of a fried chicken and a half-pan of biscuits.

Then they were through, the dishes washed and put away. Donna rehearsed her request, opened her mouth to speak. Lord reached down for his medicine kit and nodded to the bunk.

"Reckon I better take a look at you now. Stretch out here, and put a sheet over you."

"I—that won't be necessary," Donna said. "I have to be leaving, anyway. I'll see a doctor when I get to town."

"Wouldn't be very smart," Lord said, adding that the

doc in town chawed tobacco. "Dropped his cud spang inside a woman's bloomers one day."

"Mr. Lord! Will you please!"

"Gave her husband some plumb funny notions about her, not to mention the doc. Just couldn't figger out no innocent way for the chaw to've got there."

"Mr. Lord!" Donna snapped. "I am leaving here at once! If you won't take me, I'll simply have to walk!"

"It's a long walk. Reckon I better pack you up a lunch."

"*I don't want any lunch!* I d-don't want you looking at me! I—I——"

"Just doin' my perfessional duty, ma'am. Got to take good care of my lady patients."

"I'll just bet you do! It wouldn't surprise me a bit if . . ."

"If I raped 'em?" Lord shook his head. "Not the surgical cases, ma'am. Always afraid I might snag on a pair of scissors or somethin'."

Donna choked, stammered incoherently, and gave up. There was nothing else to do. The only way to stop him was to give him his own way.

She stretched out on the bunk. Lord examined her, changed the bandages, and gave her two antibiotic pills.

She was coming along fine, he announced. A little more rest wouldn't hurt anything, but it wouldn't kill her if she didn't get it.

"In other words, you think I should stay over another day. Well, I'm not going to do it!"

"That's strictly up to you, ma'am. Now, are you okay for money, or did I figure your husband right?"

"And what do you mean by that?"

"Doctorin' family sees a lot of widows. Lawman sees a lot. Funny how so many fellas are worried more about a second husband than they are about their wives."

Donna bit her lip, averted her eyes. He had no right to talk that way! As though Aaron had been mean and selfish instead of simply trying to protect her. She said so angrily, adding that her financial circumstances were her own business and that she was well able to look out for herself.

Lord nodded agreement. "Prob'ly land a job teaching good manners," he said. "Ought to get rich takin' your own lessons."

He started to rise. Impulsively, Donna put out her hand. "I'm terribly sorry, Tom—I mean, Mr. Lord."

"Tom's all right. Might break your jaw on that misterin'."

"Well, I don't have any money, Tom. I'm not trained for any job. I doubt if I could even get unskilled work, anyone so sort of old-timey and stand-offish as I am. But—but how would it help if I stayed over until tomorrow? I'd still have the same problems."

"Why, no, you wouldn't," said Lord, apparently amazed at her statement. "Danged if I ever heard of such nonsense in my life!"

"But . . . why?"

"Because tomorrow's another day! Didn't no one ever tell you that?"

She nodded; studied him uncertainly as he took the rifle from its pegs.

"But, Tom. Just how—why——"

"Why? Because, that's why! How can you have today's problems tomorrow when tomorrow's always another day? Just don't stand to reason!"

He shook his head crossly, then announced he'd have to go give the rattlers a lesson, since he could teach her nothing.

"Tom"—Donna smiled at him with unconscious tenderness—"you're not just being nice, are you? You really want me to stay?"

"Want you to stay!" Lord slapped his forehead. "Why, if I had me a wet rope, I'd whip you off'n this place right now!"

"I'll fix dinner for us, Tom. What would you like?"

"Well, let's see. A Donna Special ought to go pretty good."

"A—what's a Donna Special?"

"Now, how would I know?" Lord demanded. "It's your special, ain't it?"

He slammed out of the house.

Donna laughed softly, in strange contentment, and fell into peaceful, dreamless sleep.

18

As Lord had predicted, the problems of tomorrow were not the same as they had been today. A day's acceptance of them, a day's gain in strength, did much to reduce their awesomeness. She could smile at them—a little. She could hold them at an arm's length, studying them from all angles, assaying their weight as she tested her own strength. Since she was one and they were many, they did get out of hand. Inevitably, usually around nightfall, they threatened to take over. But when that happened, well, so much for them! Off they went into the clothes closet of another day.

It was surprising how much there was to do in a place so isolated. Baths at a tiny spring. Sunsets and sunrises to be examined. Standing, simply standing, while you slowly turned this way and that, letting the wind bathe you endlessly as you drank in the unprimped beauty of a world in its infancy. It seemed that nothing had changed here since the beginning of time. Civilization had passed it by, and the evidence was all around you. Here, in their fetal stage, were garden-variety plants. Here were animals, unaware of man's existence, ignorant of his killing proclivities. The birds could almost be fed from your hand. The huge jackrabbits reared up in your path, watched your approach with childlike curiosity. Even the cowardly coyotes were relatively brave; not relishing company, of course, but by no means panicked by it.

There was much to do, much to see, much to learn. Particularly, there was much to learn, most of it revolving around one's obligations to the Stranger. He might be a contemporary, or he might come along sometime in the future. But you must always be aware of him; whatever you did was as much for him as it was yourself. The Stranger might need your discarded tire or piece of clothing, so you draped it over a fencepost or shrub. The Stranger might step into a hidden hole or gully, so you marked the danger with a pile of rock.

Because birds were necessary to the Stranger, you lifted the fallen nest from the ground and placed it back on its perch. For the Stranger, you killed rattlesnakes; and then, because the fangs could still kill if stepped upon, you slung the carcasses over a bush. You protected the carrion-eating buzzards: the Stranger must be left with no mess. For the same reason you did not tread on the scavenger tumblebugs, the tiny black beetles who swarmed over offal as soon as it appeared, busily forming it into balls which they rolled away to their holes. The Stranger's welfare was always your concern. Always and in all ways.

Donna approved of the philosophy of the Stranger; generally, that is, she approved of it. She thought it would be a wonderful thing if everyone put it into practice, and she would eagerly join in when everyone did. Until that improbable day came, however, one had better confine the practice to a place like this, some place where its obligations were not too onerous, and where one could be reasonably sure of eventual repayment. You just couldn't do more than that, no matter how much you might want to. Help those who help you—that's what Aaron had always said. God helps those who help themselves. The meek shall inherit the earth—after the strong have taken what they want.

The last was a little joke of Aaron's, the only one he knew apparently, judging by the number of times he repeated it. But it had certainly been no joke to her, regardless of her obligation to laugh at it. She'd used to think that if she heard it just once more, if she had to laugh at it one more time——! But never mind. Aaron had been a good man, a wonderful man. And what he said was absolutely true.

No one had helped her when she needed it (except Tom, of course). No, by golly! Not unless they were darned sure of getting it back with interest, and they didn't always then! What had she got out of slaving for her father's brats? A chance for more slavery, that was all! Mrs. McBride had needed a combination maid and nurse, so she'd been given the job for her board and room, and——

No, that wasn't right. It wasn't true. She'd received much more than that: good clothes, schooling, the best medical care, spending money, everything a girl could want within reason. No one could have been kinder or more thoughtful than Aaron, even taking her part against his own wife. And—*You just bet he had!* Because his wife was dying, and he was already grooming an attractive young girl to take her place. Putting her under so many obligations, that she'd probably have kissed his—his foot if he'd asked her to. And it was a wonder that he hadn't done that, in view of all the other nasty. . . .

Oh, no! No, no, no, no! She shouldn't think such things! She didn't think them. Aaron had given her safety and security, the most important things in the world. He'd asked nothing at all, in return. She didn't have to marry him; he'd told her that repeatedly. She was prefectly free to do as she pleased. And starve to death while she was doing . . .

The days flowed together, all different, all alike. Time stood still; it raced forward; it ran backward. Time was a vehicle in an old movie, speeding ahead while its wheels spun in reverse. Today was tomorrow, and tomorrow, today. Her problems lessened, and went away. But they did not go far; she could still see their threatening shadows. But they *were* gone. And they would stay gone, unless something happened to divert her from the bright goal which was almost within her grasp. In the prim periphery of her conscious thinking, she could not admit, of course, that she had such a goal. But she *did* have it, and subconsciously, she *did* think about it. And she knew it could be managed, that she could manage it, if nothing happened. Things needed only to go on as they were for a while, and eventually she would have back all that she had lost, plus so much, much more. Everything that she had lacked in her first marriage, and that she had hardly been aware of until now. All the security of married life, plus the magic that made it worth living.

She could have it all. If nothing went wrong.

And something did.

The murder of Joyce Lakewood.

Her brutally beaten body was discovered by her landlord when he called to collect the rent. Since days had elapsed since her murder, the exact time of death—or even a close approximation thereof—could not be established. But it would be positively stated that she had died between ten o'clock one night and six o'clock the following morning.

Tom Lord had no alibi for that time.

He had an excellent motive for killing her.

19

Deputy Sheriff Buck Harris and his family lived in a five room and lean-to cottage near the railroad tracks. It was, in fact, on the railroad right of way, a circumstance which had aroused no end of joshing around the sheriff's office. Deputy Nate Hosmer claimed that you couldn't get in the door without showing a ticket. Deputy Dill Estes declared that Buck could sit in his privy and snatch striking paper from passing trains. Deputy Hank Massey stated (as gospel truth) that he had started to bed down at Buck's one night and climbed into a carload of Brahman steers. Massey went on to relate that he'd really been in trouble when he hit the Fort Worth stockyards. The suspicious pen wranglers declared that they'd heard stories like this before; they was always gettin' in a Big Sands beef that claimed to be an innercent visitor at Buck's house. And if he really wasn't a steer, how come he was hung like one? How come he had the business portion of a Bull Durham sign? Well, they had him there, o' course; didn't see no way of talkin' hisself out of *that* one. "Reckon I'd be canner beef right now, if a Association detective hadn't come along. He seen I wasn't branded proper, so he made 'em send me back."

Buck took the joshing good-naturedly, chuckling and grinning behind his hand. Maybe he felt like his pa had, that you should never mention rope in the hangman's house, but you couldn't tell it if he did. These fellas were his friends. If they weren't they wouldn't be joking with him.

He hadn't invited any of them to the house in years, but that had nothing to do with hurt feelings. It was just that he and Miss Mamie were awful short of money, and what with so many kids in the house, there wasn't much room for outsiders.

Buck stopped on the corner above his cottage, studying it covertly while he rolled himself a cigarette. It didn't look too bad, he decided. Not bad at all for a former section-crew house. He'd bought it from the railroad for a couple hundred dollars, and then practically rebuilt it. The land wasn't his, of course; couldn't own a chunk of the right of way. But there was an understanding that he would kind of keep an eye on the railroad's property, so the rent was practically nothing.

He sealed the cigarette with his tongue, closed the end with a deft twist, and tipped it into his mouth. He flicked the head from a kitchen match and touched it to the cigarette; spewed blue smoke from his nostrils.

Tilting the hat back from his forehead—a high, sensitive forehead—he reassessed the house with his fine gray eyes:

Not bad looking at all. Couldn't hardly tell what it had used to be. Look better if it was a different color, but a

193

light paint wouldn't be very practical so close to the tracks. And the railroad had its own ideas about paint. He'd had a choice of red or mucklededung yaller, so he'd taken the yellow.

Naturally that started another round of joshing. Deputy Hank Massey said the house was in the pre-zack location where the train crews cleaned out the shitters, and the mudklededung yellow was the inevitable result. "That's gospel fact," asserted Hank solemnly. "I leave to the boys here, if it ain't."

"I'll swear to it on a stack of Bibles," said Dill Estes. "Why the year afore you settled down there, Buck, they was sixteen gandy dancers killed by flying turds."

"You laugh if you want to, Buck," said Nate Hosmer severely. "People laughed at Noah when he told 'em the flood was comin', and this is per-zackly the same proposition."

Buck grinned and chuckled, a hand held over his deformed mouth. These fellas were his friends, and there was no reason to get riled. Repaint the house red? Well, that probably wouldn't change nothin'. The boys would just say that the engineer had the nose bleed, or that the conductor had the bloody piles, or—or somethin'. Seemed like they always had something to say, and he never did. He could think of plenty—he had the words up there in his head—but he couldn't say 'em. Almost seemed like they got as fouled up as them teeth of his.

It was late in the season, late afternoon of a fall day. But the weather was only pleasantly cool, and Buck's children were out in the yard. There were four of them, all girls, rocking sedately in the homemade lawn swing. The oldest was thirteen, and the youngest was six. All wore white anklets and strapped patent-leather sandals. All wore crisp calico dresses of the same pattern. Miss Mamie bought cloth by the bolt, and made the dresses up in batches. The shoes were passed on from one child to another, Buck repairing them himself. Even from this distance their mouths reflected an occasional golden glint; sparkled with the elaborate handiwork of the orthodontist. And the sight made Buck's heart swell with pride. The job was just about done for two of the girls, and in a few years more they'd all be sitting jake. Even now, even with those gold frames on 'em, they had just about the prettiest teeth you ever saw. Why those girls were so pretty, Buck thought proudly, you'd never guess they were his kids!

One of them saw him and spoke to the others. Arising from the swing, they came to meet him. They walked two abreast, since the dirt path was narrow, the youngest girls in front and the oldest in the rear. They came to a stop, beaming at him shyly, and dipped their knees in a semicurtsy.

Buck had never decided whether he should tip his hat to them, so he just kind of fumbled it around on his head. They said, "Good evening, sir," to him, and he said, "Evenin', girls," to them. (Afternoon is always evening in the South and Southwest.) They regarded one another for a moment; the girls gravely shy, Buck squirming with an excruciating mixture of pleasure and embarrassment. Then

195

the girls curtsied again and went back up the path; the youngest in the front, the oldest in the rear, the little belts of their dresses spanking them in decorous unison.

"Dawgonnit!" yelled Buck, in silent exuberance. *"Now, ain't that somethin'!"* And mentally he slapped his thigh with his hat.

Buck had worked for Old Man Billy Boy Bentley's 3-B Ranch before he became a deputy. His pa had been the ranch's smith and crumb-boss [bunkhouse custodian], and when Pa got drunk and burned himself up in his own forge, Old Man Billy Boy took charge of Buck. Buck was ten years old at the time; he'd only been to school one three-month term. But Billy Boy took him into the ranch-house parlor, sort of banging and poking him along with his cane, and handed him a book from the rows of glass-sheltered cases. "Now, start readin'," he commanded. "Start in right there where I'm pointin'."

Well, Buck couldn't read, of course; he didn't even know his A-B-C's. But Old Man Billy Boy whanged him with his cane and yelled that he was just being stubborn. So Buck began rattlin' off the first stuff that came into his mind; mixed up snatches of stuff he remembered from school.

"C-A-T spells man; G-O-D, dawg; six and nine is eleventy-three——"

"Yeow!" yelled the old man. "Hul-ly Jeez-ass!" He hit Buck over the head so hard that he practically drove him through the floor. Then, word by word, he read the passage aloud, while Buck followed the course of his pointing finger.

This above all, to thine own self be true . . .

Billy Boy interpreted the passage as meaning that a fella had better do his grabbin' and gettin' while he was still of an age to do it. Elsewise, when he became old and porely, he'd have to go around suckin' other folks' eggs (and thus be false to 'em). There was no time or no sense to crawling before you walked, or walking before you ran. You had to start running right off, without no fartin' or snortin'. "We just got this world, then the fireworks, boy. Just this world, then the fireworks, and we ain't long for this world."

By a process of memorizing, Buck learned to read before he could spell, before he had any real notion of what he was reading. He became familiar with the appearance of the words, learning to recognize them when he saw them again. And in no time at all, he was reading. Similarly, he learned practical arithmetic and the other essentials of a basic education. He was never allowed to slack up. The slightest sign of doing so brought a whanging from Billy Boy.

According to Billy Boy's own story, he'd started ranching with nothing but a satchel and a six-shooter. He'd stuffed the satchel with one hand and warded off objectors with the other; and he hadn't stopped until the satchel was full and no complainants were left. The story was approximately true, in a figurative sense. Many of the great cattle dynasties had been founded by downright banditry. Now a very old man, he frequently regretted his one-time high-handedness, and suspected its wisdom. But he still didn't spare Buck. Buck must learn to accept himself as he was, and make the best of it; and no self-pity.

"Hul-ly Jeez-ass!" he yelled, when Buck dribbled and splashed his food. "You look like a cow farted bran in your face!" And when Buck's eyes moisted a little, and his big Adam's Apple gulpily traversed his throat, Billy Boy whanged him and cursed him. "Don't you pucker up on me, boy! Wouldn't look like a tit-suckin' mule if you didn't want to! Doin' it just to spite people!"

Buck understood—mostly. The old man was helping him all he could in the only way he knew how. There was no proper dentist in Big Sands at the time—certainly nothing in the way of an oral surgeon. Anyway, the ranch was almost a half-county out of town, and months sometimes passed before anyone drove or rode in.

Miss Mamie had been raised on a small and perpetually profitless spread adjoining the 3-B. And being neither needed nor wanted there, she hired on as a kitchen flunky for Billy Boy. Buck took a shine to her right away, and she took one to him. She seemed oblivious of his mule's mouth. He seemed unaware of her one milk-eye and her slightly withered left arm. Briefly, all the elements of a romance were present, but it never came to a natural fruition. Billy Boy watched its slow blooming, and impatiently took charge. They was just about the two ugliest people in the world, wasn't they? They didn't think no one else was going to marry them, did they? Well, what the hell was they waitin' for, then?

They were married. Long before the children began to

come along, Buck was making plans to move into town. But Billy Boy was prodding him, jumping in ahead of him, before he could act. He'd spoken to the sheriff about Buck; the 3-B swung a lot of weight in the county. So Buck had himself a deputy's job.

Billy Boy tried to give him a cow to take with him, but Buck declined. His neighbors might object to a cow, he pointed out, and he didn't want to get off on the wrong foot.

During his first several months in town, Billy Boy frequently called at the house, always with some gift from the ranch. Once he'd brought a hind-quarter of beef, and another time it was two huge home-smoked hams, and another time it was something else. All this was highly acceptable to a man with a modest salary and bills that stretched into infinity. Buck acknowledged the gifts with gifts of his own: an expensive bridle, two quarts of rare whisky, and so on. And abruptly the old man stopped coming to the house.

Buck hoped he hadn't made him angry. He hoped and believed that Billy Boy had simply been giving him a final lesson, and that he'd passed with colors flying:

When anything was done for him or given to him, he must repay it in kind. He must, because he was completely without good looks and personality, without any of the traits and attributes which attract the consideration of others and serve as their own reward.

That was what the old man had always taught him: That he was as ugly as sin and as bright as hell with the fires put out. In himself, he had nothing to offer but a strong back and a weak mind.

Thus, Old Billy Boy's lesson . . . or what Buck thought of as a lesson. He never forgot it until Tom Lord came along.

Tom never joshed him like the other fellas did. Instead, Tom *talked* to him, and he talked to Tom. Without constraint, without putting his hand to his mouth, he could talk to another human being. And the wonder of it was almost too much for his inhibited hide to hold.

The fellas were always kind of hanging around Tom; a grin or a few words from him and they seemed kind of setup for the day. Yet, when he could do it tactfully, Tom would pass by the others and cotton up to him.

Buck thought it might be a mistake at first. He thought maybe Tom was just a hell of a nice guy who couldn't feel easy unless everyone else did. He thought of every possible reason why Tom couldn't really want any truck with him. And then, joyously, he at last conceded the incredible truth. Tom liked him. Tom wanted him for a friend. Tom, the doctors' son, the chief deputy—one of the smartest men in town and the best-lookin' to boot—Tom had chosen him for a friend! And why would Tom do that unless he and Buck had something in common? Unless Buck had at least a little of what he had in himself.

There was a mutual worship between Buck and his family. But it was, in the main, silent. Buck and his wife could hardly pass a "good evening" with each other without blushing. The girls conversed with one another when they were alone, but they had little to say at other times. Then Buck became Tom's friend, and the situation changed. At last there was talk. And the voice most frequently heard was that of Buck himself.

"Had a long talk with Tom Lord today," he would announce casually, as he sipped his supper coffee. "Tom wanted to know what I thought about . . ." And the girls would listen, awesome-eyed, prompting him with shy questions, as he told what Tom had said to him and what he'd said to Tom. And Miss Mamie's withered arm would twitch and squirm with pleasure at her husband's happiness.

Buck had seen the need for an R & I bureau as soon as Tom had, but he felt it would be presumptious of him to mention it before Tom. After all, Tom was the chief deputy, and it was up to him to have the first say in such matters. Meanwhile, he could be preparing himself for the time when the topic was raised, and Tom would want his opinions and help.

When it became apparent that Tom wanted nothing from him, as regarded the Bureau, except noninterference, Buck was naturally let down. But he was by no means angry with his friend. The sheriff was constantly riding Tom lately. Tom was nervous about getting everything right, and you couldn't blame him if he got a little short.

Nothing could change the way he felt about Tom. Nothing could be allowed to change it. Tom was his best friend, the only friend he'd ever had. And if he didn't have that friendship——!

Suddenly, he didn't have it.

Suddenly, it was gone, leaving a terrifying emptiness. And there was nothing to fill it but the memory of a vicious and inexcusable beating.

In his lean-to "study," Buck sat at his packing-box desk and stared dully at the pile of books on the floor. The local library, still operating on its pre-boom budget, had had none of the books he'd wanted, so he'd sent away for them, feeling a little frightened every time he bought a money order. There were volumes on criminal investigation, on fingerprinting and photography, on handwriting, toxicology, ballistics, and criminal law. One of the books alone had cost him twenty-five dollars. The total cost ran to well over a month's salary. He wished he could stop thinking about them; brooding in a way that somehow connected them insidiously with the four newcomers to town.

Ostensibly, the four were hunters—which they easily could have been. Quite a few easterners drifted out here to hunt during the fall and winter months. They had arrived in town a few days ago, and one of them had immediately become bedridden with the flu. This left the others at loose ends; so they loafed restlessly around town. Not staying together, as friends might be expected to, but each of them more or less going his own way. Talking idly to different people, buying coffee in one place, and a bottle of beer in another, and shooting a game of pool in a third. And when the sick man recovered, another member of the party became ill. So the hunters still did no hunting—except the kind they had actually come here to do.

Buck knew who the four were, just as he had known who Pellino was. He had pored over the mug books every bit as often as Tom Lord, and he had treasured every scrap of information having to do with Tom—the Highlands lease swindle; Tom's suspicions that Highlands was gangster controlled. So he knew who the four were, and why they were here. Pellino had fallen down on a highly important job. These men, his known associates, were forced to take over. The job was too big to delegate, so big that no one of the men could or would accept the responsibility for it. Otherwise, such top-echelon men as these would never involve themselves directly. And having been forced to, they would do no fooling around when they found the game they had actually come here to find.

Buck's eyes strayed again to the discarded pile of books. *To his castoff friendship.* He thought of the cost of the books—of his other and infinitely greater loss—and he thought of the four men, and their thick casually displayed rolls of bills.

Angrily, frightened, Buck tore his eyes away from the books. Huh-uh. No, by gum! He'd pay Tom off—but he'd do it himself. He wouldn't pass the job on to someone else, and take money for doing it.

There was a timid knock on the door; his wife's shy voice. "Mr. Buck?"

"Yes, ma'am . . ." Buck came to his feet. "Come in, Miss Mamie."

She entered, carrying a cup and saucer in her good hand. She said, "I thought you might want a cup of coffee, Mr. Buck," and Buck accepted it with a mumbled, "Thank you, Miss Mamie."

She looked at the books, looked away quickly. She brushed at her hair, managing to push a wisp of it over her milk-eye. Buck shifted his boots squeaking, and his hand went over his mouth.

"Is—is they anything wrong, Mr. Buck?" she said.

"No, ma'am," said Buck.

"I—I thought the j-johnnycake was kinda hard tonight. It didn't hurt your mouth none?"

"Ain't nothin' wrong with my mouth, ma'am," said Buck, a coldness coming into his voice. "It don't hurt me at all, no more."

"Uh, huh. O' course, not . . ." Unwillingly her eyes went to the pile of books. "I—I, uh——"

"Reckon you're wonderin' about them books, ma'am. Well, I'm gonna burn 'em. Be startin' me a bonfire out in the backyard any minute now. Maybe you an' me can go out and dance a hoedown around it. Ought to make a right handsome couple, don't you think?"

Miss Mamie hung her head.

Buck said he supposed she thought he ought to sell the books. She and the girls didn't have enough to eat, he reckoned, and he made 'em live in a privy and wear flour-sack drawers. "Well, don't you worry none, ma'am. I'm studyin' on getting us some money right now."

Miss Mamie nodded, shook her head. Whatever Mr.

Buck did or didn't do was all right. He couldn't help the way he was acting. He was awful, awful hurt, or he wouldn't be doin' it.

"Reckon I better go now," she said. "Y-you—you want me to tell the girls good night for you?"

"Tell 'em not to worry no more about money. Tell 'em I'm gonna buy you a arm with a hook on it, and a eye that don't look like snot."

"I'll tell 'em good night for you," said Miss Mamie, and quietly she left the room.

Buck took a halting step after her, so sick with shame and remorse that he could have died where he stood.

How could he have done that to her? Why, it was worse than what Tom Lord had done to him, and there was even less excuse for it! You might understand a man goin' kinda haywire when he was being arrested for murder. But——

Buck scowled troubledly, gave the books an angry kick. Two wrongs didn't make a right, did they? What he'd done didn't excuse Lord, did it? And those four men, the four hunters. . . .

Sooner or later, they were going to find out what they wanted to know. They had to, so they would. And as long as they were going to find out, anyway, regardless of what Buck Harris did or didn't do.

20

Donna sat on the bunk in the shack, listening to the sheriff's determinedly level voice as he questioned Tom, and to Tom's laconic, seemingly disinterested replies. She was only a few feet removed from them, but their voices seemed to come from miles away. A terrible numbness enveloped her. She was caught in a tightening circle, which at once excluded and enclosed, pinning her to a stage of her own immediate concern.

". . . about it, Tom," Bradley was saying. "You had a motive. She'd blabbed on you once, and you couldn't be sure she wouldn't do it again. Might unchange her mind as fast as she changed it."

"Might have," Lord nodded. "But it wouldn't have got her anything. Not when Mr. McBride's own widow believed his death was an accident."

"Believin' ain't the same as knowing. Miss Lakewood was a witness." Bradley shook his head. "Even if you had those two other witnesses—them oil-field workers, Curly Shaw and Red Norton to testify for you——"

Lord shrugged, said he had no idea where Curly and Red might have drifted to by now. "Prob'ly get a line on 'em, if I tried hard enough, but I reckon it wouldn't change nothin', would it?"

"Not a thing." Bradley's eyes glinted maliciously. "The way you'd see it, Miss Lakewood had done you dirt. Lied about you, when she knew better. An' you sure wouldn't like it."

Bradley had hardly looked at Donna since his arrival. He had listened to her irritably, with only half of his attention, when she had falteringly stated her conviction that Lord was innocent. The deputy—it was Hank Massey—had fastened a hypnotic stare on her from the time he entered the room. He made her feel as though he was undressing her in his mind (which was exactly what he was doing). But the sheriff's attention was wholly for Tom.

It had to be. He had little enough concentration as it was, without trying to spread it around.

". . . the house wasn't broken in to, Tom. Whoever done it, she let him in. It was someone she knew, and wasn't afraid of."

"She knew about everyone in town that wore pants. Wasn't a gal that scared easy either."

"She hadn't had nothin' to do with any other men for a long time. An' her not scarin' easy don't make it look no better for you."

"So you ain't going to look no further than me."

"Didn't say that. Might say I was just startin' with you.

You got an alibi for the time between ten o'clock an' six o'clock, and I'll start lookin' again."

"And suppose I don't have one?"

"Then, I don't have to look no more."

Donna shook herself, tried to break through the circle of dulling terror. This couldn't be happening to her! She wouldn't let it happen! Her glowing goal was too near at hand to allow it to be snatched away now.

Tom hadn't killed that woman. The idea was ridiculous—blaming him for the murder, just because he had no alibi. Why, she herself couldn't prove where she was at the time of the slaying, and that didn't mean that——

Of course, Tom *did* have a reason to kill the woman—a seeming reason, anyway. And he *would* have been admitted to the house, as the killer had been. And if he *was* capable of such a deed, well. . . .

A fit of fury. Temper. Not with a gun, but——

Donna took a small, shivery breath; she looked at the possibility and accepted it.

It didn't change anything. He was still her Tom, her beloved husband-to-be, and all that a husband represented. She was naturally dismayed that he would have anything to do with a common whore. But that was before he met *her,* Donna, and the woman had doubtless thrown herself at him and hung onto him, and—and if she'd gotten herself killed, she had no one to blame but herself! It was regrettable, of course, and she was just as sorry as Tom probably was. But it wouldn't have happened to her if she'd been a decent woman.

"Well, Tom. Got anything to say?"

"You mean have I got an alibi? How about you? Where were you between ten that night and six the next morning?"

"Now, never you mind about me! I didn't have no——"

"Seems to me that you had a pretty good motive. You was mad at her for backin' down on her story about me. And she'd have let the sheriff into her house without a struggle."

There was an angry silence. Hank Massey swung his gaze to Lord, and his hand fingered the butt of his gun.

"All right, Tom," Bradley gulped. "You're under arrest. Now just come along afore there's trouble."

"What kind of trouble?"

"This kind." Massey leveled the gun at him. "Didn't like that job you done on Buck, Tom. Just as soon put lead in your skull as not."

"Try to put about here," said Lord, tapping the bridge of his nose. "Don't like to get my hair mussed."

And then, as the sheriff stammered in angry confusion, and as Lord laughed softly, his eyes dancing, and as the hammer of the gun clicked back . . .

Then, at last, Donna broke through the imprisoning terror. "Wait!" she said, and she came forward with a rush. "Tom does have an alibi!"

Massey looked at her, let the gun slide back in its holster. Unwillingly, almost seeming to drag his head, Bradley also turned away from Lord.

"What are you doing here, anyway, ma'am. How long you been here?"

"That's my business." Donna tossed her head; and then, as he scowled at her. "I've been here since the day I was at your office. I came out here that same day."

The sheriff's eyes clouded, his thoughts blurring and drifting away in a half-dozen directions. This . . . this wasn't right. She didn't belong here, and he was going to say something about it earlier; but he'd been busy makin' a case out against Tom, an'——"

"Now, wait a minute," he said. "Last time I saw you, you was all set to kill Tom."

"I let you *think* I was. I knew how you felt about him. I thought it would be the best way of getting you to tell me where he was."

Bradley glowered, turned helplessly to his deputy; but Massey was of no help. Hank had heard of Donna, but he'd never seen her until today. He'd been out of the sheriff's office at the time of her two visits there.

Bradley's jaw set grimly. With a great effort, he regathered the scattered threads of his concentration.

"All right, ma'am," he said. "We'll just start this thing at the start. You never saw Tom Lord before you came here. Didn't know him a-tall. But less 'n twenty-four hours after you hit town, you just go t' see him, no matter what. Have to see him so bad that you pretend like you want to kill him. That what you're trying to tell me?"

"Well"—Donna hesitated—"Yes, I suppose you could put it that way. I—You see, I'd met Tom the day before, and——"

"You didn't mention nothin' to me about it."

"Well, I did, anyway! I took ill at his house and had to spend the night there. He left the next morning before I got up—it was about six-thirty, I remember, when I heard him go out—so I didn't get to thank him for his kindness."

"Ma'am," said Bradley softly. "You sure you want to go on talkin', ma'am? If you stop right now, I'd maybe forget you were tryin' to obstruct the law."

"I'm telling the truth! You'll find my fingerprints in the office of the house, and also in one of the upstairs bedrooms."

"I'll check on it, ma'am."

"I hope you do!"

Her heart was beating very rapidly, she felt flushed and breathless. A little resentfully, she wondered why Tom didn't speak up, do a little something to help himself, instead of leaving it all to her.

"All right, ma'am," the sheriff said grudgingly. "Maybe you did spend the night there. Won't say you didn't until I check. And maybe you did hear Tom leave the place *after* six o'clock by a nice convenient margin. But what about the time from ten o'clock on the night before?"

"Well . . . he was there all the time."

"Now, how you know he was? Didn't stay awake all night, did you?"

"No, of course, not! But——"

"An' it wouldn't make no difference if you had stayed awake. That's a pretty big house. Fella could wander in an' out of it without another party ever knowin'."

He waited, his face impassive. Hank Massey shifted his weight from one foot to another, continued his fascinated study of her body. And Lord remained silent; stood, grinning lazily, his eyes thoughtfully narrowed.

"Yes, ma'am?" said Bradley. "I've gone along with everything else you told me, an' it wasn't easy to do. But I'm right about this, ain't I? You can't swear that Tom was at the house all night?"

"Y-yes. Yes, I can swear to it! And I will!"

"Now, ma'am. You——"

"I know Tom was there all night b-because—*because we were in bed together!*"

Bradley gaped; waved his hand desperately as though brushing something away. "B-but, ma'am. Your husband just dead, an'——"

"I don't care! It's t-true and I'll swear to it in court, if you're fool enough to make me."

Bradley's shoulders suddenly slumped. He gave Massey a questioning look, and the deputy nodded in answer.

"It figures, Bob. After all, they're livin' together here, ain't they? No reason why they wouldn't have slept together in town."

"I guess," said Bradley dully. "I guess I don't know nothin' about people no more. Let's get out of here."

They left.

Lord sauntered over to the stove, lifted the cover from a steaming kettle, and tasted a spoonful of the contents. He smacked his lips, frowned reflectively, and turned back around. The stew tasted real good, he said, but he figured it could stand just a wee bit more salt. Not a full pinch, but kind of a baby-sized smidgeon.

Donna stared at him as though through a red haze. If the kettle had been in her hands, she would have hit him with it.

"Is that all?" she said shakily. "Is that all you have to say?"

"Huh? Oh, you mean that performance you put on. Well, that was mighty fine, honey. All things considered."

"*Mighty fine!* I lie for you, shame myself, and. . . . What do you mean, all things considered?"

"That you're pretty sure I did kill Joyce. That I maybe bumped off Pellino, too."

"I don't——" she began; and then, raging, "All right, suppose I do think that! What of it? You ought to be all the more grateful for what I did!"

"That's all you want from me, just bein' grateful? I figured it was a pretty big obligation to pay off with just plain gratitude."

"W-what? I don't now what——"

She sobbed suddenly, covering her face with her hands. She stumbled to the bunk and flung herself down on it. Began to weep uncontrollably, her face buried in the pillows.

Lord remained where he was for a long, long moment. Studying her—and himself; weighing her against himself. The balance was not greatly uneven, he decided. Not provably so, at any rate, at least at this point.

His boots clicked across the floor. He knelt at the side of the bunk and slipped an arm around her.

"Donna, honey. Listen to me. . . ."

"N-No! I w-will not! You're j-just as mean as you can be, an'—and I h-hate you! I h-hate you so much, Tom Lord, that——"

"I wish you didn't. I love you."

"I don't care! You're"—she gasped and turned around—"y-you—*love?*"

Her arms were around his neck before he could answer. She drew him down upon her breast, babbling, laughing, sobbing. "I'm s-so glad, Tom. I love you so much that I'd do anything in the world to help you, and when I tried to show you that I did—to prove it to you——W-why, darling? Why did you act as though I—I——"

"Just kind of mixed up, I guess. Might say I was plenty glad you took me off the hook, but I wasn't sure I liked your reason for doin' it."

"B-but—but I did it because I love you!" She kept his face pressed to hers. "What other reason would I have?"

Lord said he wasn't sure she had any. But neither was he completely not sure. They'd known each other a relatively short time, and there were highly unusual factors involved in their coming together.

"I was lookin' for somethin'—myself, I guess—and you helped me to find it. You were lookin' for something; in fact, you just had to have it. And I made it easy for you to take."

"Oh, you did, darling, you did! And I'm so glad I could help you!"

"Might be we helped each other too much. Maybe I'm seein' things a little too clear for comfort; maybe you ain't seein' 'em clear enough. You got your teeth into somethin' tasty, and you can't bother about who's holdin' it."

"Now, Tom," Donna said as she squirmed impatiently. "You make me sound like a dog. What possible difference does it make why we love each other as long as we do?"

Lord said that the dog wasn't a bad comparison; fit 'em both pretty well. But he figured they ought to do a little better than dogs. "Now, about that difference you was askin' about, it might make quite a bit. You're in debt to me, so to speak. I got a big obligation to you. You're pretty sure I killed Joyce, not to mention Pellino, and——"

"Now, Tom. I'm not sure of anything of the kind, and I never said I was. Anyway, I know it wasn't your fault, whatever you did. Pellino was a killer himself, and that woman was——"

"Uh-huh. But you might not always feel that. Maybe you'd decide to crack the whip over me a little bit, and I'd get riled an' uneasy like. Wonderin' if you might not go a little bit further than whip-crackin' and put my neck in a noose . . ."

"P-please, Tom! Don't talk that way."

"It could happen. Be easy for a fella that goes around killin' people out of hand. Sure, I'd had to kill 'em; just protectin' myself. But I'd see it as the same way in your case . . ."

He was speaking in a virtual whisper, a soft, shadowy tone which blended with the gathering twilight. Far, far in the distance, a coyote bayed eerily. And the night wind whined angrily at the challenge.

"Tom . . ." said Donna uncomfortably. "Maybe we'd better talk about it later . . ."

"An' maybe we hadn't. Might be too late later."

His hand had moved up from her breast. Now it lingered against her throat, around her throat, the fingers encircling the small neck, slowly, gently tightening.

"You see how it is, honey," he whispered. "Should have seen how it was all along. You knew I'd kill if I had to. You were willing to run the risk, an' now . . ."

Donna moved suddenly. Wildly. Her arms flailed frantically, and she flung herself to the floor. She backed away from him, hands shakily outthrust to ward him off.

And Lord laughed shortly. Grinned at her with a kind of wry sadness.

The blood rushed back into Donna's face. She grimaced, with an attempt to smile, and her nervous laugh became a ridiculous cackle.

"T-that wasn't very funny, Tom. Of course, I knew you were joking, but—well, after all——"

"After all," Lord nodded, "you don't know me. So I'll tell you something, for what it's worth. I didn't kill Pellino. I didn't kill Joyce Lakewood. I reckon Pellino killed her, for not following orders, but I don't know. All I know is I didn't kill him or her either, and I figure you ought to 've known it."

"But——" Donna's eyes dropped guiltily. "I'm sorry, Tom, but I don't think you were quite fair."

"Maybe not," Lord admitted. "Not to your way of figurin', anyway. It all comes back to the same proposition, I guess. We've been movin' along too fast. We got a lot of thinkin' to do before we go any further."

He put on his hat, started for the door. Over his shoulder he said that he wasn't ready for dinner yet, and that she should go ahead without him.

"I'll wait for you, Tom. You—are you going very far?"

"Nope. Just stretchin' my legs a little."

He closed the door behind him and sauntered out into the prairie. Wrapped in thought he went on, absently taking a cigar from his pocket. The dull rays of the dying sun silvered the sagebrush. Here and there a rabbit treasured this last warmth against the night, or a hunched squirrel dangled its tiny paws like a child before a cooling fire.

Lord frowned and shook his head; kicked irritably at a clod of dirt. *Lord vs Lord* were at their confusing worst today. You couldn't tell which was the ornery bastard and which the just and sensible man.

So he wasn't perfect, nowheres near perfect. Didn't it follow, then, that he should be very lenient in his judgements? Or wasn't the very opposite necessary? His imperfections had caused him no end of trouble in the past. Hardly seemed smart to compound his own with another's. And—and, hell! A fella just naturally wanted someone better than he was. If he couldn't have someone better, why have anyone? Might as well be one of those mope-pole pipe-liners, who, to quote their own joke, screwed each other and did their own washing.

Well—Lord sighed—the evidence was pretty well in; and it all pointed to a verdict of wait-and-see. And barring some decisive happening, it would have to stand there.

He found a match, started to light his cigar. In the distance there was a dim *splat!*

Lord didn't hear the sound. It was too far away, and the wind was blowing against it. He almost missed the second sound, a light thud, and the small kick-up of dust some ten feet in front of him. Almost but not quite.

Continuing to light his cigar, he kept his eyes on the dust puff. The wind blew it away, and he saw what had made it.

A rifle bullet.

21

The four hunters left town around noontime. Buck Harris stayed fairly close to them for a while, until he was sure they had taken the right road (or the wrong one) and the traffic became thin. Then, he dropped far to the rear.

There was no need to watch them. He knew where they were going, and he knew they were in no hurry to get there. They were hunters, ostensibly. So they couldn't wait too late in the day to leave town. But they'd have plenty of time to kill before their "hunt" began. In the interim, before darkness fell, they'd hole-up off the road. And the logical place to do that was the abandoned drilling well.

Buck loafed along in his old car, taking an occasional look at the speedometer. After a little less than two hours, he turned off into the prairie, followed an angling wash in the land for about a mile. He got out then, taking a pair of binoculars with him.

He took off his hat, climbed up the slope of the wash, and peered over the crest. He'd hit it just about right. He was roughly parallel with the matchstick tower that was the derrick, and the specklike buildings around it.

The binoculars were powerful—one of several pairs belonging to the sheriff's office. Buck focused them for long-range viewing, and let out a gratified grunt.

They were almost five miles away, but they seemed only a few feet. Lounged behind the bunkhouse, where their car was also hidden, they were sighting and fiddling with their rifles. Smoking and talking, and passing a bottle from hand to hand.

Buck withdrew and returned to his car. He got it back to the road and drove on toward the well. Those four were set for a while. It would be about three hours, at least, before they made a move. He could use the time to get closer to them. He could move up on them, and they—hiding as they were—would never know it.

A few minutes more, and he wheeled off into another wash, stopping, after a hundred yards or so, around a bend. He got out, picked up the binoculars and his rifle, and went on up the wash on foot. Again coming parallel with the bunkhouse, he climbed up to the crest and peered over it.

He frowned, startled. He made minute adjustments in the binoculars and put them to his eyes again. Now, from a visual standpoint, he was right in the middle of the wild-cat's installations. He could look through the bunkhouse windows, through the open door of the toolshed. He could even do a pretty good job of examining the wooded and underbrushed area to the rear of the bunkhouse. Someone might be hiding down there, but why the hell would they do it? And even though they might be hiding—which made no sense whatsoever—they could not have hidden the car.

But the car was gone. It and the four men as well.

Buck slid down the slope away; bewilderedly pondered the riddle.

"Now, let's see," he murmured. "I was five miles back the first time I stopped. Could've been gunfire and I wouldn't've heard it. Could be somethin' happened when I was gettin' back to the road, and I wouldn't't've seen it. They were out of sight for twenty-thirty minutes, an'——"

But that still didn't explain the car. If something had alarmed them into suddenly leaving the lease, they could never have made it without his seeing them. The trail from the road to the well was no highway. They could have got back to the road little faster than he had, and he would certainly have seen them. So . . .

So it just didn't make sense.

The car was gone and they were gone. That was the way it was, but it couldn't be that way! They had to be there on that lease!

Buck knuckled his eyes. He went back up the slope, reset the binoculars and began to move them in a slow arc. Bunkhouse . . . cook shack . . . toolshed . . . pipe racks . . . belt-house . . . derrick floor . . . slush-pit . . .

Buck held on the high-banked oval of ooze, feeling a squeamish twinge at his stomach. Trickles of bubbles poked up through the slimy surface and slowly sank below it. Occasionally, the bubbles combined, spewed upward in a gaseous burp, as though from a giant digesting a sickening feast . . .

Birds fell into these things. Toad and lizards and snakes were trapped in them. Small game wandered into them, and were gulped down by the slime.

The law required that the pits be filled in when a well was completed or abandoned. But Highlands spent no money unless it had to; and in the far-flung oil fields, enforcement of the law was difficult.

Buck thought grimly that it would serve the bastards right if they fell into one of the stinkin' things. And then, as he started to swing the glasses away . . .

"H-Holy God!" he said loudly. "What the . . . ?"

For the giant had swallowed too much, and now he must spew it up for another try.

Almost the whole surface of the pit was in motion, bubbling and burping and rippling. Then, there was a furious upward lunging, and the top of some object came into view. It held there for a moment, and part of the slime slid away from it, and the sun glinted on its metal top, and Buck saw what it was. And then slowly, an inch at a time, it sank back down into the pit. And this time it stayed down.

"Holy God," said Buck reverently, and it was a prayer.

Now, he knew where the car was. And probably where they were. He also knew, needless to say, that they had not arrived in the pit voluntarily or accidentally. Someone— or several someones—had put them there.

Tom Lord? Nope. Lord wouldn't be this far from his shack without a car.

It had Buck stumped. But he didn't intend to remain stumped. Whoever had done that job was still in the vicinity. He—or they—were still in the vicinity; he had to be, even though he couldn't be seen. And it was just a matter of smokin' him out.

He started back to his car, trotting awkwardly in his boots, moving as fast as the rocky wash would allow. He thought sickishly of the four men, and despite what they were he felt a little sorry for them. No one ought to die that way. And anyone who would pull a stunt like that—well, they had to be mighty low-down, or just plumb crazy.

He clambered out into the road. He was halfway across it before he caught himself. And, awareness coming to him, he reddened with anger and shame.

How dumb could a fella get, anyway? How goldanged dumb could you get?

He'd played it so danged smart. The hunters were behind the bunkhouse, unable to watch the road, so he'd thought no one else could. Hadn't figured there might be someone else there on the lease, someone hidden off to one side.

Well, the fella had had a cinch. He'd just snaked off to one side of Buck, and then circled around behind him. And good old Buck, seeing no necessity to do otherwise, had thoughtfully left his keys in the car.

The tracks of the vehicle led clearly toward town. Knowing of nothing better to do, Buck trudged wearily after them. He surmised that the hunters' car had probably been shot half to pieces in the process of killing them. So the killer or killers had another car, and had also disposed of a possible snoop. If he'd been handy, they'd probably have killed him. Since he wasn't, he'd been left on foot . . . which was practically as good, for their purposes.

Goldang! thought Buck. *Just wait until the fellas hear four people killed right in front of me. My car gettin' stole. . . !*

In his own way, Buck was a highly intelligent man, but his way was not notable for its speed. Invariably he came up with the right answer. But it took him time to do it.

Thus, for a while, he saw the clarity of the tire tracks as merely insult added to injury. The killers apparently regarded him as so dumb that they'd even driven on the soft shoulders of the road, indicating the direction they'd taken as plainly as a sign.

That was Buck's first idea: They knew he couldn't do anything, so they hadn't bothered to cover up.

Then, after another weary mile or so, the second idea hit him. *The trail was blazed one way because they intended going the other!* They'd follow the road townwise for several miles, then swing back in a wide circle to the bunkhouse. They'd been holed up around there, in the first place. Whatever their plans were, they'd remain holed up until dark. And naturally they would not head for Big Sands. Not in a car which had obviously come from there, and which might be recognized.

Buck hesitated, took a long look around him. There was a lot of distance between him and the well now. Unless the killers were equipped with binoculars as he was—and that hardly seemed likely—they could no longer see him. And they probably weren't trying to. It wouldn't seem necessary, and they'd have other things to do.

Buck crossed the road, to the side opposite the lease. Then, when he was well into the wasteland, he turned west, again moving in the direction of the abandoned wildcat.

Thirst gnawed at him. His feet seemed to be on fire. Like many far-westerners, he customarily shunned walking as a cat shuns water. He was saddle-born and bred, and he had never completely recovered from the notion that the natural function of a foot was to fill a stirrup.

He came parallel with the distant derrick. He went on past it for perhaps another mile, and then he turned back to the road, creeping and crawling for the last hundred yards.

He grasped a strand of the barbed-wire fence; he bent it rapidly, this way and that, until it snapped from the friction-induced heat. He repeated this process, farther up the wire, until it also parted. Then, tossing the resultant strand into the road, he moved on again.

In all, over a distance of less than a mile, six strands went into the dust of the road. Then, bellying down on the prairie, he waited and rested. He also felt a growing need to get some throat in his hands. Never in his life had he mauled a prisoner, but he was going to make an exception in this case. Anyone that would dump four people into a slush pit, and steal a deputy sheriff's car, was just begging for a maulin'. And they'd sure as hell get it!

It was about sundown, earlier than he had expected, when he heard the throb of his car. It was coming on fast and furious, but Buck wasn't the least bit worried. Those tires of his had about as much tread to 'em as a one-legged centipede. Any minute now that car would be taking a wild-dive into the ditch. Yes, sir, just any minute . . .

The minute passed. So did the car. With a rattling and banging of wire, it roared past Buck, the throb of its motor dimming and then dying in the distance.

Buck stood up incredulously. Then, coming to his senses, he raced for the road. No time for fooling around now, for staying in cover. That car just naturally couldn't go much farther, and he was going to be right near-by when it stopped.

At the road, he sat down and yanked off his boots. He swung them around his neck with his handkerchief, and began to run—after the car which *had* to stop very soon.

He ran sock-footed until he was out of breath. Then, after a brief pause, he started running again. He stumbled and fell down. He got his second wind, ran on and on. And . . . on.

He never knew how far he ran, how long. But there suddenly was the car, swimming before his tear-blind eyes as though it were a mirage. There was no one in it—so far as he could see. Whether there was anyone lurking near-by, waiting for him, he didn't much care. Rather, he would have welcomed the risk for a chance to take a poke at them.

His canvas water bag still swung from a rear-door handle. After a long thirsty drink from it, he checked the car's tires. Somehow, the barbed wire had got only one of them, the left front. The killers had kept going on it until it ran off the rim and the overheated motor forced them to stop. As to where they had gone. . . .

Buck readily picked up their sign: two men moving rapidly. They had crossed the ditch, and headed in the general direction of Tom Lord's shack. They were unaware, apparently, that they might be followed, believing that time would cover their trail for them.

Buck reckoned they were not calling on Tom through any happenstance. He must figure in some kind of plan of theirs; otherwise, they would have switched to the spare tire and kept on going.

Tom would need some help, Buck guessed. But he'd never be able to catch these birds on foot. He'd need the car, and if the keys hadn't been left in it—

They had been. Something else had also been left in it, too, squeezed awkwardly against the front floorboards. The bullet-riddled body of Sal Onate—so recently a member of the "hunter" foursome. On the floor beneath him was his rifle, all its bullets expended. He had been dead obviously before he was loaded into the car.

Buck unlocked the trunk compartment and hauled out his spare tire. As he set to work feverishly, he asked himself questions; and the answers poured back at him. Sal Onate had been dead when he was brought here. *But suppose he had been alive!* Suppose he had seen Tom Lord kill his friends, and he'd trailed Tom to his shack seeking revenge.

Suppose Tom was shot to death, and Onate—also dead of gun wounds—was found in the vicinity. . . .

Two men dead as the result of a gun battle: that was the picture which the real killers intended to leave.

To create it, Onate's body had had to be brought here, and Tom Lord would have to be killed.

22

Tom Lord finished lighting his cigar. He blew out the match, broke it in two and flicked it away.

Puffing comfortably, he looked around the prairie with an air of casual enjoyment. Then, completely unhurried, he turned and sauntered back toward the shack.

The bullet had come from a long way off. It would have been dangerous only with a favorable wind.

Lord entered his lean-to garage. He started his car and drove it around to the rear of the shack. He leaped out, pounded on the shutter until Donna opened it.

"Tom! What in the world——"

He cut her off impatently. "You drive a car? All right, get out of here and get going. Head for town. Follow the prairie until you get down near the road, and then——"

"But, Tom!"

"Come on! And bring me that rifle and a box of shells!" He made a grab for her as she remained motionless. "Will you move, dammit? Someone took a shot at me just now. If you don't get out of here fast, you may not be able to!"

"I—I just don't understand . . ." She shook her head bewilderedly, eyes wide in her frightened face.

Lord groaned. She was obviously too stunned to move, too shaken to escape even if he did haul her through the window and put her in the car.

"Now, listen," he said tightly. "There's a killer out there, maybe two. I didn't have time to make sure. Now I want you to leave here right now—you can still make it all right—and head for town. Tell the sheriff what's happened, and——"

"But, Tom—w-why? Who are——"

"A couple of Pellino's boys, I imagine. It doesn't matter. All that matters is that they've come here to kill me, and if you don't get the hell out of here——"

"But what about you? You've got to go with me!"

"Dammit, didn't you hear what I said? These men are here to——"

Donna said crisply that, of course, she had heard him. He was in danger of being killed. Thus, he must leave with her immediately with no further argument. "And I'll just leave the rifle here, in case you get any more crazy notions. Now, go on and get in the car, and. . . . *Go on*, Tom!"

"Huh-uh." He shook his head, eyes glinting with anger. "An' I'm gonna tell you this one more time. Because maybe you heard me, but you didn't undertand me . . ."

"Of course, I understand. These men want to kill you, and you stand there arguing!"

"I've got to stay, dammit! Don't you have enough principle about you to see that? Anyone who pulls what they're pulling can't be left running loose. I've got to take care of 'em myself, or hold 'em until the sheriff's boys get here."

"Oh, pooh! You do not have to."

"All right," Lord said grimly. "Have your own way about it. Just pitch me the rifle and shells, and do what you want to."

"No!"

He glared at her, breathing heavily. Unflinching, she met his gaze, her lips set in a firm pink line. They stood there inches apart—worlds apart—and he lunged forward suddenly and got her by the shoulders.

"Ain't learned a damned thing, have you?" he snarled. "Just can't think o' nothin' but your own sweet little ass and havin' a place to put it. Now you either get the hell out of my way, or——"

"I'm thinking about you—*us!*" She struggled in his grasp. "Just us, that's all I care about! I don't care if——"

Lord grunted that he and she had gone to different schools together. He didn't think so much of his own hide that he'd gut himself to keep it.

He tried to fling her out of the way. She jerked wildly; her shirt ripped away, and she fell stumbling to the floor, her bare breasts blooming out of the tattered garment.

Lord threw a leg over the window sill. He started to bring the other one over as she came slowly to her feet, and he jeered at her out of his pent-up fury.

"You may as well put 'em away, Toots. Maybe they'll buy you a meal ticket with some guys, but they don't mean no more to me than grapefruit."

That was all he said. It was all he had time to say. For one of her small hard fists landed on his nose and the other smashed into his mouth—as effective a one-two as he himself could have delivered. He went back through the window and fell heavily to the ground.

He pushed himself up, got back on his feet. She looked out at him, concerned but completely unapologetic, as unswervingly set on her own course as he was on his.

She said she hoped he'd come to his senses. She said she thought—didn't he?—that they'd better leave now.

Lord choked. He laughed, a little wildly, and climbed into the convertible.

Leave? *Leave?* After all this waste of precious time? After the killers had been allowed to come on, unhindered, until they were probably within spitting distance of the house?

I hope she does get killed, he thought savagely. *Because if she don't, and I get my hands on her. . . .*

He put the car in gear, raced the motor. "Tom," she called. "Tom!" As he went roaring around the corner of the shack, her frantic cry followed him, *"Tom . . . Tom, darling!"*

Night comes abruptly in far-west Texas. The pale twilight is suddenly withdrawn, and night is dropped down on the world in its place. It was night now; completely dark except for the dim beams of a weakling quarter-moon. As the convertible's headlights lunged through the blackness, the killers seemed to lunge out of it: two bearded-shaggy monsters who had waited in darkness through eternity for this one murderous moment.

They were only a few hundred yards away, coming on at a run. Lord headed straight for them, plowing over the sagebrush and rocks, jouncing high in the air as the car gathered speed.

They fired wildly, blinded by the headlights. They tried to take cover, then stumbled out of it as the lights caught them again. They threw themselves prone, beneath the full glare of the beams, and above the angry chattering of their rifles came the sound of shattering glass as the car's windshield exploded.

Lord screamed, reared up in the seat clutching himself. He fell down to the floor amidst the shards of glass, and the car careened wildly and came to a stop, its motor still running.

The killers rose up cautiously. They stood silent, listening and watching. And then one of them nodded to the other.

"Have a look. I'll cover you."

"Well . . . How about givin' him another round to play it safe?"

"Ain't got the shells to waste. Wouldn't be no surer, anyway, if we gave him a dozen rounds."

"Yeah, I guess . . ."

Lord listened tautly, mentally plotting the killer's course. He reached up cautiously, pushed the low-gear button. He took a firm grip on the bottom of the steering wheel and poised his fist above the gas pedal. And then . . .

The car leaped forward. There was a thud, an agonized scream, a furious fusillade of rifle fire.

Bullets punched through the car door. Lord flung himself against the opposite door, tumbled out into the sagebrush.

The killer was still shooting, his bullets rattling against the car as it veered crazily and stalled. Lord crawled away from the sounds, scampered back to where the dead man lay. He found the man's rifle and turned away, without giving its owner a second look. He already knew who he was. He had recognized both men from their voices, and he had been heartsick, bewildered. But there was no time for such emotions now. No time to puzzle out a riddle which could have no sensible answer.

Minutes before, in one of those hours-long moments of silence, he had heard the distant hum of a car. And in his mind, he had watched it approach, seen it stop where the trail to the shack began.

So the driver, whoever he was, was coming on on foot. And there was no reason to believe that he was anything but an enemy.

Trailing the rifle, Lord crawled back toward the car—watching as the shadows ahead of him stirred, and the dead man's companion rose up from them.

His rifle was raised to his shoulder, aimed straight at the car. He moved up on it carefully, keeping to the side and slightly to the rear of it.

And Lord moved up behind him, stopping when he was barely twenty feet away.

Then, rifle leveled at the bearded man, he stood up.

"All right," he said. "Drop it!"

Red Norton whirled around, still clinging to the gun. Lord triggered his own rifle. Frantically, he kept triggering it—and the hammer slapped harmlessly against the firing chamber.

Every bullet had been fired. He stood helpless before Norton.

Red lowered his rifle a little, and he laughed an angrily crazy laugh.

"Well, how you like it, Tom?" he jeered. "How you like bein' up the creek without no paddle?"

"I don't get it," Lord said slowly. "I thought you and Curly were my friends. You *were* my friends, dammit! Why——"

"Yeah, sure, sure. And what kind of friend were you to us? Killin' our boss! Leavin' us without no jobs and winter comin' on! Fixin' it so we'd be the patsies for a murder charge any time you took the notion. Puttin' us in the worst spot we'd ever been in in our lives, an' then just ridin' off!"

"For God's sake, Red!" Lord frowned. "What——?"

"Shut up! What'd you expect us to do, anyway? How far did you think we'd get in that old jalopy of ours, with practically no money? Well, I'll tell you, Mr. Tom Lord, seein' as you're such a good friend . . ."

They'd hardly made it into the next county, when they were forced to turn back, broke. Hadn't even got themselves a good meal or a decent drunk out of their last paycheck. And when they were still thirty miles from the wildcat, they'd had to ditch their hopelessly broken down car and walk the rest of the way.

"Had to come back," Red Norton said bitterly. "Just for a place to get in out of the weather at night. Durin' the day, when we might be spotted, we was goin' to hang out down in the underbrush. Catch rabbits an' squirrels, an' the like, an'—an'—some future, huh, Tom? A lot to look forward to after breakin' your back all your life!"

"Red," said Lord, "you should have told me you needed money the day of the accident. O' course, I knew you weren't rolling in it, but——"

"An' how would that have looked, huh? We're keepin' quiet about the killin', an' we hit you up for dough!" Norton sighed, and his voice became dull. "We couldn't do it. Anyway, we didn't figure we was so bad off at the time. Later . . ."

Norton had left Shorty at the lease, tramped cross-country to the highway, and headed into Big Sands. He couldn't flag a ride. No one would have stopped at night for anyone that looked like he did, so he'd had to tail-end it on a truck.

"I felt lower than snail shit, Tom. About as mean and low-down as a man can get. Worn-out, dirty, so hungry my belly was gnawin' at my backbone. An' now I had to pull a job of blackmail—an', yeah, that's what it was. Couldn't make it come out no other way, so I swallowed it an' it didn't set too well. It did somethin' bad to me. Me and Curly had a cinch on you, and you'd have to pay off.

And . . . and then I got to thinkin'. We didn't have no more on you than you had on us. We'd left the well after you did. You could claim you'd never been there, and with Joyce to back you, you could probably make it stick . . ."

He didn't think that Tom would be that dirty to 'em. Tom was their friend, a guy who had always treated them tops. On the other hand, look what they were doing to Tom, and they'd always been *his* friends.

Killing changed people. Pressure changed them. And if Tom was squeezed too hard, or thought he might be . . .

Red was almost relieved when he found Lord's car missing from the driveway, and knew he was not at home. But he had to have money, a few bucks at least. So he'd gone on over to Joyce's house, thinking the deputy might be there.

Lord's car wasn't in front of the house. Nervously, not wanting to bother Joyce unnecessarily, he'd crept around to the rear to check the garage. And Joyce came up behind him and shoved a gun in his back.

"She was plenty burned up, Tom. Reckon she had a right to be, too. You'd threatened to kill her if she caused any trouble, and she'd caused plenty. And she was all set to give you some more."

"Now, wait a minute!" Lord protested. "She——"

"I'm tellin' you," Red said stubbornly. "I'm tellin' you what she told me, and I could see how she felt."

Joyce wouldn't believe that Red had come there to find Lord. She was convinced that Lord had sent him to kill her. And she jeered Red for his supposed stupidity.

"You and your good friend, Tom. Hah! You know what would have happened after you bumped me? Well, you were scheduled to be next, you and your pal, Shorty!"

She marched Red into the house. She intended to turn him over to the sheriff, but in reaching for the telephone, she turned away for a moment. And Red slugged her. He kept slugging her.

It was her or him—wasn't it?—and that was no choice at all. She had to be silenced. By killing her, he was also gettting rid of Lord, for Lord would certainly be blamed for the murder.

"I had to do it, Tom. You see that, don't you?"

Lord said he guessed he couldn't. But he hadn't been in Red's place. Red said angrily that Lord was damned right about that!

"I took her gun with me, threw it away while I was tail-endin' out of town. Took me until the next afternoon to get back to the well, an' the way I was feelin', I just couldn't take no more. Just one speck more o' trouble, and I'd be blowin' my stack. An'—and then . . ."

There'd been more trouble. Plenty more.

Shorty hadn't meant any harm. He'd started off by kind of teasing the "fat fella" (Pellino), trying to throw a scare into him like you could with a greenhorn. Then, he got another idea: to take the guy for his money and his car. They could drive the car back to their own, switch license plates, and be a couple of states away before the alarm was out. Lord would probably guess that they were involved in the robbery, but no one else knew they were back here. And Lord was in no position to talk.

But . . . but then Pellino had got himself killed in the snake nest and Shorty, panic-stricken, and trying to dispose of any evidence, had run the car into the slush pit.

"Too scared even to tell me," Red said tiredly. "Prob'ly wouldn't have known about it, if he hadn't broke down an' started bawlin'. An' me, I kinda broke down, too. Because now we were really in the soup. . . ."

Pellino was obviously a man of importance. There'd be a search for him, and to attempt flight would only draw attention to themselves.

They'd felt no better about their situation when they discovered that Lord was staying at his shack. To them, it was proof that his influence was still strong, that he'd been able to squeeze out of the frame into which Joyce's murder had put him. Everything was Tom's fault—all their terrible peril and misery. Yet Tom was living high off the hawg with a girl friend, and they had to skulk around like coyotes. Jumping at shadows. So damned sick and scared that they could hardly eat the little grub they were able to get.

"Couldn't see but one way out," Red went on. "Didn't look like nothin' was going to be done about Joyce's death; not as things stood, anyways. So all we had to do was nail you for killin' the fat guy, and we had it made. We could go on hidin' at the lease for a while, until everything had cooled off. Then, we'd show up in town, like we'd just blew in . . ."

He paused wearily, rubbing a hand over his face. Then, as Lord tensed himself to spring, the rifle snapped up again.

"Don't do it, Tom. Gonna happen soon enough, anyway. O' course, if you're in a hurry——"

"No hurry at all," Lord said hastily. "Suit me fine if you talked forever." And he listened intently, tried to penetrate the darkness around him, as Norton continued.

Red had made no mention of a third man, an accomplice. So the man who had stopped down there in the road could be a friend. Someone, at least, who could help in this otherwise hopeless situation. For Red certainly intended to kill him. As soon as he had vented his hatred orally, rationalized the crimes he had committed and was about to commit. . . .

". . . about all, Tom," Red concluded, telling how he and Curly had disposed of the hunters. "Guess we wasn't real smart, kinda screwed everything up, but then we never claimed to be bright. Ain't like some people that make trouble for their friends, an'——"

Lord cut in on him sarcastically. Obviously, there was nothing to be gained by sympathy, but he might buy some time with an argument.

"You pore, pore fella you! You've known for years that cable tools was on the downgrade. Jobs were disappearin' like snowflakes on a hot stove, and you don't do nothin' about it. Won't have nothing to do with rotary rigs."

"You're damned right!" Norton snarled. "I'm no mud-hog! Me, I'm——"

"Yeah, sure. You're a cable-tool man, a rope-choker. So that's what you're gonna be, even if you wind up with a rope chokin' you! A man with a boy's head, that's you. Can't do nothin' but bungle and blubber. If you could, you wouldn't be in this spot!"

"Uh-huh. An' what about the spot *you're* in?"

"I'm stupid, too. If I wasn't I'd 've known you were."

Red whimpered angrily; he urged Lord to keep it up and see what happened. "Gonna get me somethin' out of this deal, Tom. Me an' your girl friend's gonna have a lot of fun together."

"You mean you are, don't you?" Lord drawled. "Can't see a puny little fella like you tacklin' a ninety-eight-pound woman while she's still alive."

Norton didn't get the ugly joke for a moment. When he did . . .

The rifle leveled and steadied; he looked down the barrel of it, his finger tightening on the trigger. "Turn around if you want to."

"Not me," Lord said. "My papa told me never to turn my back when I was close to a horse's ass."

And he flung himself forward as one last rifle shot rang through the night.

23

Red Norton shifted his bandaged arm in its sling and signed the confession which Donna had taken down. Buck Harris folded it and put it in his pocket. He and Lord helped the injured man into Buck's car. And Lord asked if Buck was sure he could manage by himself.

"With two of 'em dead?" Buck shrugged; and then he lowered his voice a little. "What about this fella, Tom? What do you reckon they'll do to him?"

Lord said he wished he knew; he kind of had Red on his conscience. "Prob'ly what should have been done long ago. Put him someplace where he might be helped, and he can't do harm."

"Well . . ." Buck scuffled his feet. "You positive your car'll run, Tom? Looked pretty shot up to me."

"It'll get me into town, anyways. Go in with you right now, if you like."

"No hurry. Prob'ly better if I go on ahead and clear things up with Bradley."

Lord nodded. He held out his hand awkwardly. "I hardly know what to say, Buck. I——"

"Ain't no need to say anything. After all, we're friends, ain't we?"

"You know it," Lord said fervently. "If you hadn't winged Red when you did——"

"Me?" said Buck. "That wasn't my shot, Tom. Couldn't get one in from where I was."

"Yeah?" Lord frowned. "Then . . . Oh, yeah," he said.

"Uh, it ain't none of my business, Tom, but would you mind telling me somethin'?"

"Practically anything but my own name. I ain't sure I remember it right off."

"I mean, uh, about her. How come she seems right t'home here, when she was dead set on killin' you?"

"I don't know," Lord sighed. "I guess I'm just unlucky."

Buck drove away.

Lord stayed where he was, absently massaging his jaw—looking up into the night, as the slender moon fattened and grew full, and the stars pressed eagerly against the azure window of heaven.

Well, he thought. *Well, what if she had saved his life? It was her fault, was it not, that his life had had to be saved. Except for her selfish attitude, her insistence that he ignore everything he lived by—*

The door behind him opened suddenly. With very awkward suddenness, since he was leaning against it. As he pitched backward into the room, Donna caught him by the elbow and jerked him erect.

"Now, what are you doing?" she said severely. "Haven't you had enough nonsense for one day?"

Lord pulled away from her. He said she was to get changed into her woman's duds, and be quick about it.

"You're gettin' out of here," he added. "I'm takin' you into town tonight, and you ain't comin' back."

"I see," she said. "You have it all settled, do you?"

"Reckon I do, yes, ma'am. I just found out it was you that took care of Red out there, and maybe I ought to be grateful to you. But——"

He broke off as she turned and went over to the stove, began ladling stew into two plates. Placing them on the table, along with bread and butter, she sat down and began to eat.

Lord hesitated, fidgeted, and sat down across from her. "Now, looky," he said. "I told you we was goin' into town. We're leavin' right now."

"Eat your dinner," Donna said. "I've warmed it up about fifteen times now, and I'm not going to do it again."

"And I'm not going to tell you again." Lord's eyes glinted dangerously. "You get switched into your store duds and do it quick, or I'll do it for you!"

"That would be typical of you," Donna nodded, spooning stew into her mouth. "When you can't win an argument through reason, you resort to force."

Lord scowled; this was definitely a very low blow. Even the Plaintiff Lord, of the legendary *Lord vs Lord*, had never filed such a sweeping charge.

"All right," he said. "We'll reason—if you know how.

244

I'll tell you how I look at things, and you just show me where I'm wrong."

Donna said that was fine with her. "Now, hadn't you better eat, dear? Or can't you do it while you're reasoning?"

Lord snatched up a spoon, took a huge mouthful of stew. It was boiling hot, and he choked and sputtered, his eyes watering. Donna buttered a slice of bread and handed it to him.

"Eat that with it, dear," she said gently. "And maybe you'd better take smaller bites."

Lord accepted the bread shakily. He took a very small bite of the stew.

"All right," he said. "We'll take it right from the beginning. For a marriage to work, people have to have a lot in common. You'll agree to that, won't you?"

"No, I won't."

"But—but you got to! Everyone knows that!"

"I don't," said Donna, and she looked up at him levelly. "Believe me, Tom, people can have a very miserable marriage and still have a great deal in common."

"Well . . . well, look, now," Lord said. "You want a home, comfort, security. You do want that, don't you?"

"Of course. Don't you?"

"Well—uh—to a degree, yes. But they don't mean everything to me."

"They don't mean everything to me, either. The only thing that really matters is love. And"—she gave him another level-eyed look—"you can believe that, too."

"All right!" Lord pounced on the statement. "But how

can you love a man when you're hell-bent on changing him? Tryin' to make him knuckle under to you like you tried to tonight. I was only doin' what I had to do—couldn't face myself in the mirror if I didn't—and——"

"And I tried to stop you. I loved you that much."

"Love? What kind of love is that?"

"My kind. And it isn't the kind that you think it is, something that measures everything in terms of a bank balance and a full belly. If it was, I wouldn't have tried to stop you, because I knew how you'd feel about me. I knew I'd probably lose you, and I loved you enough to do it anyway."

"Well, now . . ." Lord hesitated uncomfortably. "I—uh——"

"I tried to protect you. When I couldn't do it one way, I did it another. I took the rifle that I wouldn't let you take, and I went out there where I didn't want you to go. And—a—and"—her voice broke briefly; became firm again. "But that was very wrong of me, wasn't it, Tom? That was very selfish of me. It proved that all I was looking for was a meal ticket and a place to sleep."

Lord couldn't think of much to say to that. He couldn't think of much, period.

Donna arose suddenly, snatching up the plates from the table and carrying them over to the corner washstand. After a moment, her back still turned, she said she'd change clothes as soon as she'd done up the dishes.

"I think you're right, Tom. We couldn't make a go of it. It's best that you take me into town tonight."

"Well," Lord said. "I ain't so sure about that."

"I think you must be. You couldn't have said the things you did unless——"

"Dagnabbit!" Lord yelled, smashing his fist down on the table. "Why didn't you stop me from sayin' 'em, then? Gonna stop me from doin' things, why didn't you do that?"

"B-but. . . ." She faced him timidly, the beginning of hope in her eyes. "But, Tom——"

"Don't 'but' me! You wasn't on the job, was you? Wasn't lookin' after me like you're supposed to?"

"No, Tom," she nodded meekly. "I'm sorry, Tom."

"Well, you ought to be! Lettin' all sorts of things slip by you. Why"—he pointed to the bunk—"just look at that bolster there! You let me put that up, didn't you? Wouldn't bother you a bit if I got bolster bumps, one o' the most insidious diseases known to man."

Donna assumed an expression of horror. She said something would have to be done about the bolster right way, and she would be glad to assist.

"I'll run out and get the hammer, Tom."

"I'll get the hammer. You just get them dishes cleared up, and make a big pot of strong coffee."

"C-coffee? But I thought—won't it keep us awake?"

"You're doggone right it will," said Lord enthusiastically. And as Donna blushed to her hair roots, he went out for the hammer.

He knocked the bolster loose.

She made coffee.

He threw the bolster out the door.

She poured coffee.

They drank the coffee together, and they blew out the lamp together. . . .

And in the far-west Texas night, in the incredible, heart-breaking beauty of the night, peace came to Tom Lord and Donna McBride.

VINTAGE CRIME / **BLACK LIZARD**

___ **Carny Kill** by Robert Edmond Alter	$8.00	0-679-74443-6
___ **Swamp Sister** by Robert Edmond Alter	$9.00	0-679-74442-8
___ **The Far Cry** by Fredric Brown	$8.00	0-679-73469-4
___ **His Name Was Death** by Fredric Brown	$8.00	0-679-73468-6
___ **No Beast So Fierce** by Edward Bunker	$10.00	0-679-74155-0
___ **Double Indemnity** by James M. Cain	$8.00	0-679-72322-6
___ **The Postman Always Rings Twice** by James M. Cain	$8.00	0-679-72325-0
___ **The Big Sleep** by Raymond Chandler	$9.00	0-394-75828-5
___ **Farewell, My Lovely** by Raymond Chandler	$10.00	0-394-75827-7
___ **The High Window** by Raymond Chandler	$10.00	0-394-75826-9
___ **The Lady in the Lake** by Raymond Chandler	$10.00	0-394-75825-0
___ **The Long Goodbye** by Raymond Chandler	$10.00	0-394-75768-8
___ **Trouble Is My Business** by Raymond Chandler	$9.00	0-394-75764-5
___ **I Wake Up Screaming** by Steve Fisher	$8.00	0-679-73677-8
___ **Black Friday** by David Goodis	$7.95	0-679-73255-1
___ **The Burglar** by David Goodis	$8.00	0-679-73472-4
___ **Cassidy's Girl** by David Goodis	$8.00	0-679-73851-7
___ **Night Squad** by David Goodis	$8.00	0-679-73698-0
___ **Nightfall** by David Goodis	$8.00	0-679-73474-0
___ **Shoot the Piano Player** by David Goodis	$7.95	0-679-73254-3
___ **Street of No Return** by David Goodis	$8.00	0-679-73473-2
___ **The Continental OP** by Dashiell Hammett	$10.00	0-679-72258-0
___ **The Maltese Falcon** by Dashiell Hammett	$9.00	0-679-72264-5
___ **Red Harvest** by Dashiell Hammett	$9.00	0-679-72261-0
___ **The Thin Man** by Dashiell Hammett	$9.00	0-679-72263-7
___ **Ripley Under Ground** by Patricia Highsmith	$10.00	0-679-74230-1
___ **The Talented Mr. Ripley** by Patricia Highsmith	$10.00	0-679-74229-8
___ **A Rage in Harlem** by Chester Himes	$8.00	0-679-72040-5
___ **The Name of the Game Is Death** by Dan Marlowe	$9.00	0-679-73848-7
___ **Shattered** by Richard Neely	$9.00	0-679-73498-8

VINTAGE CRIME / **BLACK LIZARD**

___ **Kill the Boss Good-bye** by Peter Rabe	$9.00	0-679-74069-4
___ **The Laughing Policeman** by Maj Sjöwall and Per Wahlöö	$9.00	0-679-74223-9
___ **The Locked Room** by Maj Sjöwall and Per Wahlöö	$10.00	0-679-74222-0
___ **The Man on the Balcony** by Maj Sjöwall and Per Wahlöö	$9.00	0-679-74596-3
___ **The Man Who Went Up in Smoke** by Maj Sjöwall and Per Wahlöö	$9.00	0-679-74597-1
___ **Roseanna** by Maj Sjöwall and Per Wahlöö	$9.00	0-679-74598-X
___ **After Dark, My Sweet** by Jim Thompson	$7.95	0-679-73247-0
___ **The Alcoholics** by Jim Thompson	$8.00	0-679-73313-2
___ **The Criminal** by Jim Thompson	$8.00	0-679-73314-0
___ **Cropper's Cabin** by Jim Thompson	$8.00	0-679-73315-9
___ **The Getaway** by Jim Thompson	$8.95	0-679-73250-0
___ **The Grifters** by Jim Thompson	$8.95	0-679-73248-9
___ **A Hell of a Woman** by Jim Thompson	$10.00	0-679-73251-9
___ **The Killer Inside Me** by Jim Thompson	$9.00	0-679-73397-3
___ **Nothing More Than Murder** by Jim Thompson	$9.00	0-679-73309-4
___ **Pop. 1280** by Jim Thompson	$9.00	0-679-73249-7
___ **Recoil** by Jim Thompson	$8.00	0-679-73308-6
___ **Savage Night** by Jim Thompson	$8.00	0-679-73310-8
___ **A Swell-Looking Babe** by Jim Thompson	$8.00	0-679-73311-6
___ **Wild Town** by Jim Thompson	$9.00	0-679-73312-4
___ **Web of Murder** by Harry Whittington	$9.00	0-679-74068-6
___ **The Burnt Orange Heresy** by Charles Willeford	$7.95	0-679-73252-7
___ **Cockfighter** by Charles Willeford	$9.00	0-679-73471-6
___ **Pick-Up** by Charles Willeford	$7.95	0-679-73253-5
___ **The Hot Spot** by Charles Williams	$8.95	0-679-73329-9